Save Your Own Life

Save Your Own Life

Kansas Stories by **Amy Sage Webb**

WOODLEY PRESS
Washburn University
Topeka, Kansas

Acknowledgments

The following works, sometimes in slightly different forms, have previously appeared in the following publications:

"Communion" — *Midland Review.* "Helping" — *Red Rock Review.* "How It Goes," "Union," and "Born in October" — *Eclipse.* "Lost and Found" — *Clackamas Literary Review.* "The Wedding Gift" — *Tahoma West.* "Animal Control" — *Fourth River: Journal of Nature and Culture.* "Prairie Paradox" — *Flint Hills Review.*

Cover image reproduced by permission of the artist:
"Your Seat Cushion May Be Used as a Flotation Device," by Ann Piper, acrylic on canvas, 1998

Author photo by Stephan Anderson-Story, 2012

Book design by Leah Sewell | lsewell.tumblr.com

Woodley Press

WOODLEY PRESS

Washburn University
Topeka, Kansas

The Bob Woodley Memorial Press
Washburn University Topeka, KS 66621
(785) 670-1445
washburn.edu/reference/woodley-press/index.html

Other Titles from Woodley Press

Mythology of Touch
Mary Stone Dockery

This Ecstasy They Call Damnation
Israel Wasserstein

Kansas Poems of William Stafford
Edited by Denise Low

Begin Again: 150 Kansas Poems
Edited by Caryn Mirriam-Goldberg

For Michael, best and last

Contents

Born in October – 13

I.

How It Goes – 17
Communion – 27
Union – 27
The Memory of Water – 38

Prairie Paradox – 57

II.

Helping – 60
Animal Control – 79
Forty-Six Pounds – 82
Lost and Found – 94
The Wedding Gift – 103

Born in October

As long as a dammed creek rams up
        the walls of a well,
post rock fissures, clefting the prairie in its fist,
and a hedge row anchors
        the shadow of a blue heron stalking
        shallows by a bridge,

As long as nests of mud-daubers
        thick on the barn
        empty their stores of spiders,
crops lift in the bellies of birds,
and a clock ticks the hours of days,

As long as there is a soldier
        returning to the battlefield where he lost
        an arm or a leg,
a lover, toasting an empty glass,
a mother stitching
        the pattern of grief in a quilt
        for a dead child,

Then I will know my own image in this life.

I am not the tooth,
        or the space in the gum that was the tooth,
I am the place in the mouth to which the tongue returns,
        the chorus of coyotes calling the end of night.
I am the razed field gleaned to silage.

And if the sky thickens with the silk
        of milkweed floss broken loose
        and spun in skeins of gold light,

If the howl of a barn cat torn
        by a great owl's hunger wakes you
                to the skitter of mice in the walls
                and the call of geese
                        veeing a blue-black gash in a red horizon,

Then the dogs will bare their teeth and snarl the scent
        of buck-rown cedars stripped white,
and a winter of wind
        will carry the curse of your breath
        across an open lament of snow.

I am the echo recalling the voice
that tells the story of autumn children,
        how we tear late into this world
        through the belly of summer,
        the iron taste of blood
        still singing in our mouths.

I.

While studying allergies in 1984, Jacques Benveniste, M.D., research director at the French National Institute for Medical Research, observed that when highly diluted solutions, or homeopathic remedies, were administered to allergy systems, the systems reacted as if molecules from the active ingredients were, in fact, still present. In other words, it appeared as if water retained some trace of the active molecules. This controversial theory has since become known as "the memory of water."

Nature vol 333 (1988)

How It Goes

—The Café—

Brett Ralph is at the point he hates in relationships. It is at this point that love songs he hears on the radio seem to pertain to him, and he cannot drive to work in his truck without imagining scenes of himself and Amy June. Running toward each other in a field, walking arm-in-arm along a deserted beach. He has never done such things, but he is beginning to visualize them each morning in the pre-dawn darkness of his windshield, choreographed to the songs he hears on KZON. They are at the point right now where she is getting up with him and sending him off with coffee and egg sandwiches wrapped in foil, and he knows it can only get worse from here until she dumps him. It will take effort on his part, as always, but she will drop him like a hot stone. He smashes his fork down through the crucial bite of his custard pie, causing the remaining parallelogram of custard and crust to fall backward. The point of pie-librium. You always get there. She is going to leave him. He knows it. Just like that.

—The Woman—

Is too good for him. She teaches high school. She rarely speaks in contractions. She grows herbs and vegetables in her yard. She composts or recycles everything it is possible not to throw away. She knows the answers to whatever questions he asks her, like what is the difference between saccharin and NutraSweet. The fact that Brett has only a GED does not bother Amy June.

"Some people know things from books, and other people know things hands-on," she says. "They're just different types of learning," she tells him, when he brings it up, which is often. In response to this he tells her, "I think you kinda like me bein' the way I am, don'tcha?"

Amy June does not mind holding his hard hat and his auto-security Club when she rides in his truck. She seems concerned for his tools. She has suggested that he buy a better bolt-on steel box for the truck bed.

Brett pays for his custard pie and coffee, then stands chewing a toothpick while he talks to the cashier. Her name is Dianne. She works the lunch shift at the café near the site of the new office complex where Brett is hanging sheet rock, a southwest-themed place called El Rancho.

"Hey Dianne," Brett leans across the register toward her. "Can I get a cup of ice from ya? Just a cup or so. I forgot to put ice in my cooler this mornin'."

She tells him sure thing and brings back a stainless steel bowlful of ice. "You take that out there and fill it up, and bring me back the bowl, okay honey?"

"I got a meatloaf in there, and I don't want it to go off, you know?"

She stands with her hands on hips, the way waitresses can do. "Food in here not good enough for you, huh?"

"Well, you know." Brett shrugs. "My girlfriend made it for me. We gotta work overtime tonight and she made it for me for dinner. I just don't want it to go off in the heat and all."

"Well how about that. A meatloaf. That's nice. What's your girlfriend do?" Dianne asks as Brett elbows the door open to the blue-early light of the parking lot.

"She works at Burger King," he says. "She runs the Fry-A-Lator."

— *The Meet-Up* —

Was six months ago. His brother Vincent had been fussing over a pan of some kind of noodles and sauce when Brett appeared at his apartment and asked for a place to stay for a few days. With his back to Brett, Vincent scraped a plateful of grated white cheese onto the pan, covered it with foil and shoved it into the oven.

"A few days," Brett said, leaning against the door frame, neither in nor out of the room. "I got my stuff in storage, see? Fucking roaches everywhere. Fucking roach motel."

"This is not a good time. I am entertaining, Brett." Vincent stood with his hands on his hips in a very feminine way. "Can you see that?"

Brett sniffed and backed away onto the landing outside the apartment door. "I'm just tryna get myself set up out here, ya know?"

Inside, hands still on his hips, Vincent stared at him through the narrow galley kitchen and the open front door.

"I figure I'll have to bomb it," Brett said.

"Bomb it?"

"The storage locker. Two or three times." Brett held his forefinger and thumb cocked like a gun, and exhaled cigarette smoke over them. "Nuke em from orbit."

"A couple days." This was not a question. Vincent wiped his hands on a soft-looking towel and stared pointedly at Brett.

"A couple days." Brett dropped then ground the cigarette butt under the heel of his boot.

"And stay outside." Vincent began pulling plates from a cabinet. "I have people coming over for dinner."

Two hours later, outside on the living room balcony, Brett smoked his way through a pack of cigarettes while sipping from a giant plastic cupful of soda. Inside, Vincent and his friends laughed and ate at the dining room table. A man in a sport coat had asked, but Brett, noticing Vincent's back-and-forth hands gesture behind the man's back, had refused to join the party. He preferred to keep Vincent's apartment a "smoke-free environment," Brett said, smiling grimly at Vincent from the balcony. Now he sat watching. Occasionally, when one of the people inside looked his way, Brett lifted his head back in a kind of nod, acknowledging in case anyone could see him out there in the dark. When no one nodded back, it occurred to him that the eaters could see only their own reflections. The thought at first irritated him, but as he watched, he began to feel a secret and guilty pleasure. He observed how the man wearing the red tie opened the wine and poured it, how the brown-haired woman dropped her spoon and did not notice.

Then she came to him. Amy June, the one he had been watching the most. The other two women wore pants. This girl was wearing a sleeveless yellow dress. Brett had seen her take off her sandals and set them on Vincent's coffee table as soon as she arrived.

She slid the patio door open just enough to slip through, and shut it behind her so that the sound of conversation and music faded to near silence. Overhead, a jet thundered by, and along the balcony railings, maple branches and soft leaves whished back and forth. Brett nodded across the darkness at her.

The woman sighed and leaned into the wind and leaves. "It's nice out here," she said. "Might even rain tonight."

In the light from the dining room window, he could see the line of her back beneath the dress. The white spot lighting on the apartment grounds illuminated the profile of her face. On his side of the balcony, still dark, Brett lit a cigarette.

She turned to him. "Can I bum a smoke?" She tilted her head sideways in a very pretty way. She had black hair, pulled in a knot at the nape of her neck. Her skin was very pale. This was a pretty girl.

"Things'll kill ya."Brett lit it for her as she leaned forward toward him.

They sat in lawn chairs opposite one another, smoking silently.

"Lemme move those outta your way." Brett stood suddenly and pulled his work boots from beneath the chair where she sat. He set them carefully beneath his own chair, tucking the socks so that they stuck out the tops. "I don't wanna stink you out."

"I hadn't noticed," she told him.

At some point, he managed to find out her name was Amy. Last name June. Amy June, which made them sort of alike, he pointed out, both having last names that were first names. He introduced himself as Vincent's brother. Sort of the black sheep of the family, he told her. Something like that. That's why she might not have noticed him around much.That is, if she hung around Vincent much.

"Yes, I do." She leaned back in her lawn chair and drew one leg up to brush dust from her toes. "But Vincent doesn't know I'm alive."

In the dark, Brett smiled to himself. "Beautiful girl like you? Come on. My little brother must be goin' blind not to notice you."

"Well maybe he is," she said.

"Yeah, maybe. But then, Vince is a pretty good lookin' guy himself, ya know?" He leaned toward her, into the light. "Come to think of it, both of us are. We're a good lookin' family. Whaddaya think, huh? I look a little bit like Bogie? I get a trench coat and a hat?" He rubbed his thumb across his upper lip and then lit another cigarette. "Here's lookin' at you, or however it goes."

"You and Vincent do look sort of alike," she said.

She smiled.

She had fallen for his shit.

He had her.

—*The First Lie*—

"What do you do?" She asked him.

"I'm in the construction business."

"What do you build?"

"I like to build churches and schools." He sat leaning into the light on her side of the patio, hunched over in his lawn chair and looking up at her seriously. "It's such a competitive business. I like to build things that help people, you know?"

"Really? I teach school. At Rosemont. They have a new wing. Did you build that?"

"Well no. Not that one. I haven't been working this area very long. I been workin' around the East Coast a while. Just relocated back to the Midwest this year. He turned his profile to her and stared at the maple branches scraping the railing. "It's important to be near family."

"You mean Vincent?"

"Yeah. Since our mom passed, you know." He paused. "We got our differences, but I think me and Vincent got a special kind of relationship, you know?"

—*The Bad Day*—

After his morning pie break at the café, Brett works straight through his shift at the El Rancho complex until dinner. The problem is not the hours. The hours are good. The problem is that Brett is working with the fat man. The guy is nice, but he's fat. Really fat. And he keeps eating baking soda all day for his digestion, which bothers Brett because the bag, sitting there on the Jolly lift, looks like a big bag of cocaine or something. Brett imagines the foreman coming by and seeing him standing there next to the bag of powder. It infuriates him, but there is nothing he can do. His job today is to wheel the Jolly lift along the wall where the fat man is working the screw gun. That's it. Just push the lift, which is stupid enough even a monkey could do it, though that is no easy job considering how fat this guy is. Brett looks up at him. He hates him for being fat, and, when the foreman walks by a moment later, Brett hates the fat man even more.

"How's it goin' Ralphie boy?" The foreman claps him on the shoulder, and Brett winces. He is never sure if the foreman makes this joke knowing that Ralph is his last name, or if the foreman thinks his first name is Ralph. If he gets called by his last name, the foreman is ribbing him. Other guys get called by their first names. If the foreman thinks Ralph is actually Brett's first name, then it just goes to show how outside the loop he is, because he's been here eight weeks. By now they should know what his name is—should have seen it on his hard hat, his tools. Brett pushes a pack of cigarettes down deeper into his shirt pocket and nods at the foreman. Nothing, he thinks to himself, is fair.

"Everything okay?" The foreman looks up through the crossbeams of the Jolly lift at the fat man, and, Brett thinks, at the bag of white powder and teaspoon sitting on the control box next to him.

"Yep. I don't think he's doin' so hot today, though." Brett nods up at the fat man.

"Oh yeah?" The foreman leans toward Brett accusingly. "You telling me you're not gonna get this section finished tonight?"

"No, nothin' like that. I was just thinkin' he's not doin' too good. I think his stomach's actin' up. He's been eatin' a lot of bakin' soda for it."

The foreman barks a single syllable laugh. "Ah, Marcus'll handle it." He moves away toward another section of the building that is now undergoing wiring. Brett cannot tell if he even saw the white powder or not. Above him, the fat man bangs the crossbeams to let Brett know it is time to wheel the lift a little further along the section of wall they must complete with screw-gun studs tonight. Brett thinks on and off about seeing Amy June after he finishes at the site and has gone for a few beers. She will be warm and asleep, and will probably answer the door in one of those long shirts she wears.

— *The List* —

Amy June gets up to let him in, though she has a meeting at seven in the morning, she says. Brett removes his boots and socks, and places the socks in the boots. He places the boots under the chair on which he is sitting, next to his tabloid newspaper. He rinses out a Styrofoam cup in the kitchen sink and tells Amy June that he's brought it so she can put his coffee in it in the morning. He asks her if he can take a shower.

"Don't use my face soap," she says.

He forgets to bring the other soap into the shower with him, and uses the face soap anyway. His hands make dark gray whorls on the white surface. After his shower, Amy June uses the bathroom and comes out with the soap in her hand. "Brett," she says, "didn't I tell you not to use this?"

He apologizes. He pulls a towel around himself and asks her if she has anything to eat. He opens the refrigerator and stands staring into it for several minutes. He asks if she can make him something to eat. He asks her if he can do some laundry. He drops his work clothes into the washer in a whiff of plaster dust and asks Amy June would she scratch his back? Some dust got on him. When the laundry is done, he asks her will she hang it on the line for him? He doesn't have any clothes to wear outside but the towel.

"What time did you set the alarm for?" Brett asks her when they are finally settled down between the sheets of her soft bed with all the pillows and the brass headboard.

"Three-thirty," Amy June says sleepily.

"Better make it three."

"Why?"

"So I can hit the snoozer a few times."

"God, you have to be joking." She pokes him. "You think I am going to listen to that thing wake me up every ten minutes for an hour? No thanks, Buster. You get up too early as it is."

He can hear that she is smiling. She does not seem quite as tired as she did a minute ago. Brett knows they should have a joke about this, about the way he always hits the snooze button, about his faults. But, he thinks of the dark windshield he will be looking through in a few hours, driving again. Driving past the neighborhoods and strip malls on dark highways toward the fat man and the Jolly lift and the bag of baking soda on the control panel.

"Would you just do it?" He snaps at her.

"Oh, Christ." She sets the alarm and turns the light off again, then settles into her pillow, hard, not touching him. They sleep all night.

In the morning, Amy June gets up and makes coffee, which she brings to Brett in bed. He insists he cannot get out of bed without it, but it does not wake him. He falls asleep again and tips the cup over onto the beige carpet. A half hour later she reminds him that he must get up. It is almost four. He tells her to just leave him alone and stop nagging him.

—The Worst Part—

She didn't make him any breakfast. Like it would have killed her. Brett Ralph is late. He cannot drink the coffee he bought at Stop-N-Cop for at least twenty minutes, it is so hot, by which time he is irritable. When he goes to the café for morning break, he tells Dianne how tired he is of working these twelve-hour days. "I make good money. But, you know," he stares purposefully up at her from the booth, "sometimes it seems like this business is nothin' but greed." He leans back and lights a cigarette while Dianne stands there topping off his coffee. "Money can't buy happiness, like they say."

Dianne nods. "You know it, honey. It sure can get you close, though."

Brett sits and smokes through the beginning of his shift. The fat man will be coming back about now, he imagines. Brett does not even look at the tabloid he bought at Stop-N-Cop. Across the restaurant, Dianne is dropping a filter into the coffee machine.

He figures Amy June makes just about the best egg sandwiches of anyone. He could do without those little slices of tomato she always put on them, though.

—The Way It Goes—

Three months later, Amy June has transferred to another school, and Brett Ralph is at the point he hates in a job. It is at this point that the bits of conversation he overhears on breaks between the foreman and the other guys begin to conjure images in his head. He pictures the new tools he will be hauling out of his truck every morning. The steel-lined box he will build to lock them up on the next site. He does not own any of these things yet, but he cannot help visualizing them, as he visualizes the foreman staring up at a particularly good piece of finishing and clapping him on the back. They are at the point where the El Rancho job is almost finished. The company will be moving to another building. It will not be his fault, as always, but the company will not renew him. The money-grubbing bastards. Things can only get worse from here.

Brett Ralph goes to his brother's apartment again when the guys he is rooming with in the motel near the building site get drunk early and lock him out.

"A couple days," Vincent tells Brett, standing on the apartment landing with his arms crossed in front of the door. "That's it."

"Couple days, bro, I'm outta here. I shit you not."

Two weeks later, Brett is setting his alarm for 3:30. He winds the clock and sets it next to the futon next to which he has set his boots, inside of which are his rolled-up socks and cigarettes, all of which are next to the patio door in case of a midnight smoking emergency because, you know, you never know.

"Hey, Vince," he says. "You need to get yourself a girlfriend, man."

Vincent snorts disdainfully and turns out the lights in the kitchen, where he has just finished washing a stack of dishes. "There's an extra blanket on the couch if you need it, and the regular coffee is in the refrigerator. The special kind is in the freezer. Don't use that, okay? You don't even like it. And if you need salt for anything—I can't imagine what would require salt at three in the morning—"

"Three-thirty."

"Whatever. If you need salt, use what's in the shaker." Vincent holds up a cylindrical box. "This is new salt. Don't open this. And don't forget to lock the door when you leave in the morning."

"Jeez! All right! I will shake the salt habit. I will be sure to drink the right coffee and lock the door, Vince." Brett pulls a sleeping bag up over his head.

"Look, I'm sorry." Vincent leans against the wall of the hallway. "I'm just tired. I wasn't expecting you to still be here, and I need to get good night's sleep tonight."

Brett pulls the sleeping bag off himself again.

"Oh yeah? Big day at the office tomorrow?"

"Not exactly."

"Not exactly?"

"No. I'm going out of town. Gonna try to visit somebody."

"Well that's good. You need a vacation prob'ly, huh?"

"Maybe." Vincent switches on a small nightlight in the hall and turns to go. "Just going to check in on a friend."

"Female friend?" Brett pulls himself into a crouch and begins fishing in his boot for his cigarettes.

"Look, Brett, you can't stay here while I'm gone. This is the last night. I mean it."

"I understand, bro. You'd rather have this whole place sitting open and your flesh and blood out on the street." Brett begins to pull his socks on.

"No. Look." Vincent holds both hands to his head. "It's not like that."

"It's all right. I know when I'm not wanted." Brett pulls his boots on and begins slowly to lace them.

Vincent stands wearily in the hallway, rubbing his hands against each other. "Look, just stay tonight, all right? Just—stop what you're doing. Just quit."

Brett stops and stands there with one hand on the patio door. "I just asked what friend you're visiting. I worry about you sometimes. You never have a girl over here."

Vincent grimaces. "Yeah, well, you might have met her over here once. She used to teach middle school near here and then she transferred to a better district. More benefits. In Colorado."

"Mm. Colorado. That's tough. But, you know. That's how it goes, I guess." Brett opens the door a crack and lights a cigarette, blowing the smoke outside while still standing in the room. Behind him, Brett hears Vincent's knees pop as he turns toward the bedroom. It is funny how, in the glass, Vincent appears to be in front of him, receding into the dark backdrop of the maple branches and the balcony outside.

"Yes. She was great, though. She was an incredibly nice woman. I miss her." Vincent sighs and trudges out of the halo of the night light.

"How it goes," Brett Ralph says to himself as he slides the door shut behind him and stands on the balcony, looking out into the shapes the tree branches make of the spotlighting against the building. Yes, he thinks. The way things go. People turn, disappear. Everything. Just like that.

Communion

When she talks long distance to her boyfriend in Atlanta, Allys refers to these women as "my friends." When she listens to them speaking to one another at the club, Allys does not know what to say.

To Allys, the skinny woman speaks of shoes. They are attracted, each woman, to the white leather, the zany piping of each other's footwear. They shout at one another over music. It begins in August when a clot of women gathers on the curb outside the blue doors on a Saturday morning. Bab Rourk, the manager, is late opening. A fresh morning after rain. Women in bright clothes, bright litter blown by a storm, waiting. When Bab opens the doors, a host of crickets, amassed in the foyer through the night, spill forth onto the sidewalk and the waiting row of white shoes. The women, howling, chase crickets with hand weights. Beside her, Allys sees the skinny woman's foot come down, crack, upon a cricket's back. Teal insoles. Purple laces. Allys notices, but she is new here. She waits.

Nothing happens.

November. Allys is the first to speak. November already, and Allys has said almost nothing to anyone but the students in her classes, who listen to her talk about literature for fifty minutes, three days a week. She imagines herself halved by the podium in front of them, droning on. In November, the skinny woman is warming up in front of Allys for a class called Get Fit. Nobody is getting anything at the moment. Rows of women shift back and forth, white shoes purling the shag carpet, pulling up knots of detritus from classes before. There are fingernails. Old hair. No one vacuums in the Awful Aerobics club. Allys does not even think of it by any other, even its actual name anymore.

"Crosstrainers?" Allys ventures this noun.

"Yeah. I like 'em." The skinny woman looks to the floor, to Allys, who raises one knee then the other. "Them crosstrainers too?"

"Yes." Suddenly, the months of solitude like cracked clay in her mouth, and what feels like a hemorrhage of words: "I have the running shoes too. I used to buy another kind, you know, and I was really loyal to them. But then I tried these one time, and I got hooked on them. I went and got the running shoes too." An awkward second of silence follows. Too much too quickly, Allys knows. She holds up one foot to show the design on the sole.

The skinny woman crouches to see, remains down for a squat thrust. "Only shoes I ever had was Wal-Mart shoes. Then finally I went and said the hell with it. Bought myself a pair of Nikes." Pronounces it in one syllable, like pike. "Never go back to the other ones now."

Allys nods, thinks of the rows of shoes in her closet. Noses of shoes waiting, like obedient dogs. "I know," she says, immediately regretful of initiating conversation. Allys feels as she does when she asks a friend to go somewhere with her and the friend is busy. One of the things Allys likes about her boyfriend in Atlanta is that he will go anywhere with her. He never has anything better to do.

The room, a slab of cold air. Everyone just standing, killing time.

The manager, Bab Rourk, is explaining the November club contest. She gestures to a card table stacked with Tupperware and various home and beauty promotional items. This month's contest, construction paper cutouts inform the class, is "Let's Talk Turkey." A paper fold-out turkey with a crease in its neck stares at the women in profile with one beady eye. It has replaced October's ghost with mechanized arms, which called out Ooooh! Ooooh! with increasing insistence throughout each class.

"You bring in two canned goods, and that gets you registered for the contest. Then you'll get one of these little cards." Bab waves an index card and gold pencil at the rows of women who are rubbing their arms and shuffling behind the long, hand-hammered woodbeams that serve as platforms for Step aerobics. Nervous stalks of corn. Bab's ten steps to winning the 28 pound turkey and five free tans tuft them this way and that. Allys thinks of the tanning bed, of the hand-markered sign taped to the glass sarcophagus: Caution: Ultraviolet Radiation. Below these words, the admonishment: Tan Fat LOOKS Better Than White Fat. Allys fights the urge to ask Bab whether the winner can combine the five free tans with the turkey and bake it in five consecutive sessions. She bends forward and stretches her hamstrings. Stares at the carpet.

"And the money goes to the Salvation Army to feed the needy." Bab concludes in a gasp and slaps a notecard onto a stack alongside the Tupperware.

At the front of the room, the Get Fit instructor punches down a silver tab on the tape player and thukking, ringing aerobics music bleats out of the speaker that is suspended above Allys and the skinny woman by two thin chains. These attach to the foam ceiling tiles with eyehooks. Shaky, Allys thinks. The speaker reverberates with a sound of no quality but its loudness. The Get Fit instructor's voice, a tinny puncture through it like a tattoo needle: Grapevine left. And knee.

The speaker on the right side of the room supplies only midtones. No bass, no lyrics. The women on that side lean toward Allys and the skinny woman's side. The room lists like a ship offkeel.

The skinny woman in front of Allys adjusts her headband as class begins, bright yellow on her dark hair. Tugs bike shorts the color of sour milk down over her straight thighs. She is all sinew and knobs. The long bones of her legs and arms, beige-white and narrow as pared soap.

Over the music and the instructor's staccato, the skinny woman's voice, thrown over her shoulder at Allys like a terra cotta shard: "But I like your shoes though. You got to tell me where you got those."

December. Now they talk of shoes. Amazing—the soles, the laces and padding—things that can be done with shoes now. Today the instructor, Jamie, stalks to the sauna after class, coughing. Bab, at the front desk, pencil ticks along a list of women who have paid their monthly club dues. The skinny woman flips through magazines while five women, bright-faced with stepping, zip into jackets and drink from the cooler. Suddenly, she spins toward Allys. "Are these the best you ever seen, or what?"

In the photo, the shoe of a six-foot-three women's NBA forward. On the sole, a blue rubber tread in the shape of a fish. WNBA. White shoes with blue fish soles. Allys agrees. They are the best she's seen.

The skinny woman smacks the magazine down into a wire rack on the counter triumphantly, as though she had stitched the shoes herself.

"Reeboks," she says. "You ever had a pair a them?"

Allys nods yes. Stops before the words, Lots of them.

"They're way too expensive though," the skinny woman continues, conspiratorially. "I priced em. You can get you a pair of Nikes for less out at Boorman's. But Boorman's don't carry Reebok. I asked."

Allys nods. Imagines her future at the Awful Aerobics club: a solid row of Nike hightops with fishless soles.

On the phone earlier this morning, Allys's boyfriend tells her that she does not have to live out here, you know. When her contract is up in May, she does not have to renew it.

"It can't be so hard to teach college that you have to move to the middle of nowhere," he says. "There are schools all over the place."

"So what if I was there?"

"Here?"

"Yes. Say I'm still in Atlanta."

"It'd be great."

"Oh, yeah?"

Yes, he tells her. Yes.

"Tell me what happens."

She hears him sigh. "What?"

"We're in Atlanta and I'm lying here on my couch talking to you. I say, Hey, why don't you come over."

"Yeah. That'd be great if I could."

"So you're coming over right now. And what do you bring me?"

"I don't know. What am I supposed to bring you?"

"I don't know! Something."

"Like what?"

"Like I don't know. Maybe you bring me a six pack of beer. Or an article you cut out of the paper. Maybe you bring me a gallon of ice cream and you sit there and feed it to me where I'm lying on the couch. In the sun. The sun in streaming in and you're feeding me chocolate almond ice cream with a big, round spoon."

In the club, the women have all pulled on sweat pants and gloves now. Before she can leave, the skinny woman must fetch her daughter from the nursery.

"Boo!" she yells in the direction of the Plexiglas square, behind which a smaller version of her, black hair, no headband, pounds a plastic truck against the wall. To Bab Rourk and the other women who stand gossiping around the orange cooler she stage-whispers, "It's her birthday today."

A thud against the paneling, as though Boo will bludgeon her way into the aerobics room. This nursery, a perfect square of paneling and plywood, bearing waxy testament to boxes immemorial of colored crayons. In the center of the scribbled walls, the Plexiglas window overlooks the rows of wooden benches where the women step up and down. Boo appears fiercely in the window again, suspended by one arm in the grip of a fidgety pre-teen wearing a college sweatshirt. Boo presses her nose and lips to the Plexiglas, a wet pink polyp blossoming.

"Now that's really attractive." A comment tossed over her shoulder, toward Allys. "Boo! Come on." The skinny woman is holding a small blue jacket out in front of her.

Suddenly, a black-haired child butts her way through the slabby bottoms of the women, their red hands and white water cups. Sidestepping and butting at her mother who holds the jacket outstretched, Boo prances the length of the aerobics floor, a small goat hopping up and over the beams.

The skinny woman, speaking in the full italics of motherhood—"I said today is her birthday." This, ostensibly to Bab, but loud and out the side of her mouth, like a funnel aimed at the child.

As if catapulted from across the room, Boo is immediately among the women again, shouldering into the outstretched parka, zipping it herself.

"I'm gonna get presents!" The voice lighter than the mother's, as yet unroughened by puberty and cigarettes.

"Well now!" Bab pulls back the glass patio door which separates her office, like the nursery, from the aerobics room with a window and paneling. She scuttles out again with a shopping bag. "My nephew's birthday is today too. You wanna come to that party? You wanna crash a party, Boo?"

Boo looks at her mother, whether pleading for permission or release, Allys cannot tell from the doorway where she is buttoning her fleece jacket.

When Allys thinks of the city, her back aches. The three syllables, at-lan-ta, throb at the base of her spine like a kick in the kidneys. In one of the Hemingway stories she teaches at the local college, there is a line when the woman says to the man, That's all we do, isn't it? Travel around and try new drinks? What does it mean? The students stare at her dully, heavy as Angus cattle. There is no describing it to them, these students who have never really experienced a large city, about how it is there, how there is always something to do.

In Atlanta, Allys thought of the Midwest. She thirsted for quiet and weather. Imagined, hungrily, the great spaces between everything and everyone. Allys did not imagine livestock and mobile homes. Relentless wind. Angle parking. Or the way the featureless Midwest would take her breath and voice out of her. The way, out here, she would find nothing big enough to say. When she hears herself speaking, everything Allys has ever done seems to have happened to some other person. At night, Allys listens to the blues hour on the radio. Singing along with Bessie Smith, then Etta James, she hears her own voice at last: Steady and clear and freighted with someone else's life.

She is about to leave the club, but Allys sees Bab Rourk pull two white plastic blobs from the paper bag she is holding.

"Know what these are?" Bab waves one in the air and turns it upside down to reveal a candy cylinder adhesed with tape.

The women around the cooler cock their heads in different directions. No one can guess. Allys can see by the squinched knots at the navels that the white shapes are balloons. Fleshy red points extrude from their tops. They come like that, Bab says. Red and white balloons. You don't blow up the red part. Only the white. Leave the red ends standing up.

The skinny woman eyes Allys knowingly. "Well you know what they look like, don't ya?" She holds one of the balloons in her hand and twangs the red protrusion with her finger.

"Oh for goodness sake!" Bab pick up the other, patting its bottom where the candy is taped. "They are Tootsie Roll trolls. See? You tie a Tootsie Roller here, and this front part makes the face." To the skinny woman: "That is the nose." To the others: "And you let your kids decorate em like so." Bab traces with her finger, two dots and a semicircle. "They can draw their own faces on."

The women agree these are the cutest, and where does Bab find the time? Allys thinks of Bab. Bab running the women's fitness club. Bab chairing the Early Bird Optimist Club: "Funding activities to keep kids off the streets." Bab each weekend wearing striped coveralls and conducting the miniature train ride at Soden's Grove. Bab on Wednesdays wearing a red satin windbreaker stitched with whit pins and bowling a 287. Allys does not understand Bab at all.

"Easy breezy," Bab speaks to everyone. "Get yourself a craft magazine like one of these we got laying around here, buy your supplies, and in an hour or so you got a kid's party. Easy."

It now occurs to Allys that another of Bab's endeavors is a children's party service. Clearly, there is nothing Bab cannot turn into effective promotion.

Allys thinks of her own small house, of the mile she will jog from the club to get home. On the drainboard in the kitchen, a papilloma of spreading circles: cups, plates, saucers, and bowls. Not even space on the counter to assemble a sandwich. Only Allys's vigilance about her food, unflagging. When she finishes lunch today, Allys will write down the calories and fat content of each item in a journal she keeps on top of the refrigerator. In Atlanta, her boyfriend never eats breakfast. This bothers Allys. She remembers mornings of waking him with slices of toast, bagel halves. He could forget to eat, he tells her. He really could.

Outside the Awful Aerobics club, Allys breathes deeply, noting a cold tinge in the air but the wind gone milder. A day of bright sun presaging, everyone says, snow by midweek.

"Hey, take care now!" It is the skinny woman, holding her daughter by one hand.

Allys nods, hidden already behind her sunglasses.

"Don't let yourself go and catch that thing Jamie's got. I had it. It's wretched."

"I won't."

"Hope not, with her hacking around in there. Gross in' it?"

"Yeah." Allys shrugs her shoulders, implying, What can I say?

She watches the skinny woman back a stuttering white panel van away from the curb, Boo bouncing on the passenger seat. An earsplitting backfire and black fart of exhaust and they are rattling away with a wave. No license plate in back. A spare tire cover bearing an NFL logo, and a bumper sticker in the dusty back window: Camel Cigarettes.

The sun, air, water purling along the curbs, all reminiscent of a recent thaw, though the snow is yet to come. People shopping move, anesthetized, in and out of storefronts. Allys begins slowly to jog. In front of her an old man wearing washed-out tans: tan jacket, tan shirt, tan pants with a knifeblade crease, leans against the brick front of the drug store. Shaves ash from his cigarette by plying it to the storefront. Tips his hat at no one. Tan hat, Allys notes. Of course. Halfway down Union Street, two boys unload something from a dolly. Allys is alongside them before one calls to her.

"Hey! Waddaya doing?"

She turns, jogging in place. One of her students. One she likes.

"Nothing." Allys is abruptly aware of herself, a red jacket standing on the sidewalk. A ponytail swishing, a gloved fist gripping a sweat-sodden yellow sports bra. She is a caution sign. With her free hand she pulls her bulbous wraparound sunglasses closer against her face. Purple reflective shades. Insectile. She feels ridiculous. "What are you guys doing?"

The boy shoulders a forty pound bag. "Working." Smiling, he is across the street, he and the other boy gone between angle-parked cars into the meandering Saturday traffic. On the dolly, next to the truck with an open side door, Allys sees five more bags: Dog Diet, in black letters. She shades her eyes with one hand, watching the boys cross the street under bags of dog food. They enter a carpet store.

This town!

Allys begins to jog again. Across the railroad tracks everything quiets. The steel doors of the autobody shop remain scrolled down this morning for the weekend. No country music. No clanking of metal parts, hiss of compressed air. Saturday morning. Even the EconoWash Laundromat is relatively quiet, most of a row of empty washers lid-up like urinals. The Bait Shop is a little blue house on the corner of Union and South. High-pitched roof and four clapboard walls, Dr. Pepper sign and three words in black paint on the north side: Bait Reels Tackle. On the west side, facing Union, three different words beside the screen door: Shad Sides & Guts.

A rising wind bears Allys the smell of cooking meat. She breathes shallowly, cautiously scenting for the boiled-blood smell of the beef processing plant blowing from the west. The flatulent smoke of the soybean factory to the east. North of town, the doughnut factory, billowing with sugar and lard. Ahead, Allys sees the hamburger and pie shop, its chimney pipes steaming. Inside the window, an elderly couple spooning milkshakes. Allys remembers her boyfriend sitting with her on the front porch of her house in August. He, visiting. Two old people walking by.

"Look at that." He, next to her on the porch swing, looking out at the sidewalk. "They still hold hands."

The sign outside the burger shop has not been changed since Fire Safety Awareness Week: Never Leave Your Cooking Unattended. A low-slung blue car rattles and shakes in the drive-through lane, receiving a fat white sack. Allys's mouth fills with salty saliva. Her muscles burn against the cold and the rhythm of jogging, the impact underfoot of the sidewalk flags. She thinks of her refrigerator: Skim milk. A foil-covered plateful of cooked yams.

In the burger shop, Allys sits at the counter and orders cherry pie. There are fourteen varieties here. But, a man sitting next to her with a Gazette tells her, you can't go wrong with cherry. The pie is warm and flaky and oozing with fruit and sauce. Allys spears the cherries with her fork, one at a time, and swirls them in a melting ball of vanilla ice cream. When he looks up to wave at the waitress for more coffee, Allys asks the man next to her for the sports page.

December. Football season. Not nearly as interesting as baseball, Allys tells him when he asks her what team she is following. She says nothing of Atlanta, the Braves.

"I'm waiting for spring training, honestly," she says.

He nods his head at her. Puzzled, perhaps impressed.

About thirty-five, she thinks. Dishwater blond hair and blond-brown stubble on his face that probably goes reddish around the mouth when it grows out some. Work-worn. Wearing the Midwestern Uniform: Boots with rawhide laces, low-slung jeans, a sweat shirt and baseball hat that is not, never out here, turned backwards. Around his eyes, a cicatrix of puckered lines that stretch deep when he smiles.

She feels words. Nascent, rising. Then, "I went to KC for a couple Royals games this season, actually. I'd go more, but, you know. Work."

The man nods appreciatively. "I do know."

Allys watches the lines around his eyes.

"You just come from there?"

"Oh, no." She looks down at herself and smooths her jacket over her legs. "I work—" she scratches a drip of ice cream from the spandex of her running tights with her fingernail. "I mean, I'm not working today. I'm off."

"That's the way," he says. "Not much better'n some coffee and a piece of pie on your day off, I'd say."

Allys folds back the first page of the sports section. She can feel him looking at her. "Actually, if you want to know the truth," Allys smiling, the words aimed like a spear toward the space between the stranger's eyebrows, "it's my birthday today."

"No kidding?" He smiles. He tears the tops from two plastic capsful of creamer and stirs them into his coffee with a red plastic straw.

"No kidding."

"So you got big plans then, hmm?"

His coffee must be half milk, she thinks. "Maybe," Allys says. She traces four lines across the ball of ice cream with her fork. "I'm trying to decide between a couple of things."

Allys plucks another cherry from the pie and forks it to her tongue. Sees, outside the windows, a gust of wind lifting two letters from the shop's sign. Three-quarters skyline and a smudge of tan grass, nothing of a view. Allys watches the sun go dim then bright again under passing clouds like a fritzing bulb. The man beside her asks Allys if she would like a cup of coffee.

"It's on me," he says. His smile again. Allys, tilting her head to one side.

There will be snow. Allys can imagine it: great patterns of wind and cloud, swirling over distance. Large, blanketing. She winces at the sour-sweet pleasure of cherry in her mouth. This town, being what it is. Some weather, so simply unavoidable.

Union

I'm standing on throbbing feet, the toes of my boots lipped over the floor drain of the Union Bar and Grill. Tony Shylo, the old man in suspenders, has gone in the back to count money, then to sleep with his head propped against a case of Old Overholt. Pussitari is with me in the front. His shirt, open to the ribs, his St. Christopher medal slung low to clank against the glasses of girls he hopes to take home.

"S.O.B. gets more ass than a toilet seat," Tony always says of Pussitari. But there are no girls to take home tonight, Christmas Eve. Outside a light snow, and only Nancy Boone at the counter. Nancy pushes a bill and change toward me. Orders a Shaeffer, though I know she hopes I'll make her a B-52: vodka, Kahlua, milk, and Bailey's Irish Cream. All the serious drunks look to complicated concoctions on Christmas Eve.

I pull a Shaeffer from the cooler and push her money back at her. Cracking the beer, I set it before her and say, "Tis the season." My own small gift.

"Ain't but two season around here," Nancy croaks. "Rain an' construction. I don't care for it."

She pulls a long draw from the can, her white throat working. Nancy Boone, pickled at a flat-line forty. Pale driblets of blonde hair. Her balding and ratty fur coat. She shakes a Pall Mall from a crumpled package and lights it, blowing smoke in a hard, straight line that unravels before me.

The smoke, unribboning. A woman, a fur coat.

I am thinking of my mother before cancer. Tipping the flame of a gold lighter to a Salem. The rich sheen of her coat in the amber glow of hallway lights. We are standing in the atrium before the opera begins. "You could be very good," she says, "or very average." Inside, my father waiting, the program on my mother's empty seat beside him. She, in front of me, hands over a clutch of bills. Her hair, in the light, red as a house burning down.

A reflection superimposed over the night street: Pussitari and I, in tee shirts emblazoned with the Union Jack, the all-but empty bar. I could have been anyone. Anyone at all.

And what if in this moment, Pussitari turns to me, pulls the St. Christopher from his chest and drops it into my palm—says, "Here. You. I pick you." And the years unravel before us into ashes, my hips thickening. He will go fat in the throat and thin in the legs. A prostate problem. A need for low-fat foods. Pussitari and me, locked in the solid and steady death of marriage.

Here in the bar we are light as paper, moths in this strange, uneven light. Christmas Eve, 1983. The years, this season, accruing behind us like so much snow that fell too softly to stick or do anything with.

The Memory of Water

I.

Blood-flecked and foaming, the horse in the exhaust tube pummels forward in a blind speed as if its own life recedes before it. Trina holds the bridle attached to the nose cone-tube while the horse's head lifts higher with each forward stride. She digitally raises the speed of the treadmill a notch, a notch, until the horse runs at thirty, forty miles per hour while she stands beside the treadmill with the syringe. The hooves and machinery in the corrugated steel trailer beat a deafening whir around her. Pieces of loose dirt and stones fly back from the treadmill and shatter against the back wall of the trailer in a spray against the sign that warns, "Do Not Stand Behind Treadmill. Beware of Flying Objects." Drops of sweat fly from the horses' flanks, spattering Trina's eye goggles. She tastes the salt of this spray on her lips. By the end of this night she will emanate the sweet, sweat-stench of horses, their hairs and dirt filming her skin, the remembered rhythm of their hearts beating beneath her hands.

Even you equine people, her fellow veterinary students tell her, have to get out sometimes. The town south of the vet school sparkles with holiday lights and the stadium speakers ring with carols. On this night, Trina thinks, she might shower in the locker room, might go down to the college bar district later, be among people. But where? With whom? Beyond the experiment trailer, the stables, and the winding drive home to her small rented cabin, Trina really has nowhere to go.

It is called alveolar lavage, this infusion of capillary-opening antihistamines and pure oxygen pumped into the horse's lungs as they run. The horses Trina loads onto the treadmill and buckles beneath their bellies with a giant garter are called bleeders. Genetics, partly. They are race horses, bred to run and continue running, the capillaries in their lungs bursting, their nostrils foamed with blood. Breckmeier's hypothesis is a proven fact by now. Lavage will keep even these retired, donor horses alive and running at speeds in excess of their best track times. The question now is how long. It is Trina's job to run the donor horses until they die or become too crippled to run.

For the horses, the running and the living are the same thing. She leads them halting and side-stepping each day to the treadmill in order to understand. Blood. Genetics. What happens to a flesh divided against itself? The horses have learned the sound of her truck, and each morning as Trina drives the winding dirt road to the trailer, she can hear them whinnying and kicking at the steel sides of the barn. By the time she has lifted the cinder block beside the door and found the key to the experiment trailer, they are a riot of hooves and screeching. They want to run. They want to run until they die.

In the cavernous trailer, Trina works alone this night behind windows rimed with frost. Her breath clouds. The horse's body steams. Wheeled carts on either side of the treadmill beep and pulse with numbers and graphed lights. Trina checks the heart rate monitor, the resistance monitor, the flow meters and the I.V. tubes running overhead from the catheter in the horse's neck to the blood station. Slowly, a notch, a notch, she reduces the speed, watching the corresponding numbers on the monitors. Trina grips the bridle close to the horse's face for control. This is the most dangerous time, when the horse can slip. Its weight might break the garter. The horse could fall to one side or the other, breaking a leg or worse. Just last year a girl from Lucas tried running on the treadmill after hours. She was still mangled and unable to walk, people said. The space between the conveyor and the metal plates is large enough for an arm, a leg, a lot of things to be pulled through. Trina has felt the weight of this in dreams, a horse slipping from her, a bridle pulling through her fists.

Tonight the conveyor paces down flawlessly, the horse slowing to a walk, its sides heaving. This horse is Algorithm. A stupid name for a horse, Trina thinks. Academic and un-swift. She walks the horse down, pressing her thumbs into the damp flesh beneath the clavicle, timing the beats. The heart rate is high, on the monitor, beneath her hand. She pulls the plunger from the catheter in the horse's neck and shakes away the plug of dried blood, pulling until the new blood begins coursing into the syringe and up through the tubes overhead to the station. When he is bled and the catheter capped off again, Trina runs her hands over the horse, speaking to him not in words but in sounds. She blankets him and backs him carefully from the treadmill and over the metal plates, then through the corridor to the arena. Algorithm is still coming down slow, his heart an unsteady ratchet inside his ribs. Trina paces him around the dressage ring in the empty twilight. The peated earth, the hush, the barrels to one side. Not the close, searing tang of dog piss and cat pheromones in tiled cubicles, but this smell of peat and large animal flesh in the quiet ring. Trina is forty-three years old. She specializes in equine veterinary work for these moments, this feeling alone.

The horse's pulse should be steadying now. Trina runs one hand along its flank, holding the horse's head at the bridle.

"Come on now, boy. Sweetie pie." She coos to the horse, soothes her hands over him. "Calm down now. Let's get a cookie. Let's get a cookie and a brush. We'll brush you out, boy."

She will douse the horse's meds in molasses and feed them to him with the special pellet meal. She will brush the slick hide until it shines. Trina will stand in the horse's stall with her face against its neck this night as she does each night. "Come on, boy. Come on."

But Algorithm skitters away from her, then lunges as she holds to the reins. Trina lunges the horse several more times, allowing him lead and charging him around her, the center of this small circle inside the large, brown blankness of the ring. The horse's eyes are rolling, and even at this length of lead Trina can see its heart-pulse knocking against the flesh of its chest. The catheter tube flips loose from its tape and flops against the horse's mane and heaving wet sides. Algorithm's flesh twitches all over under the skin, as if beset by biting flies. The horse is having some kind of seizure. Algorithm. Twelve years old. Ancient by horse standards. Weak of hip, flank-scarred by bites from a herd-bound mare named Blainey. As the horse goes down, front legs first, the hips raised strangely for an instant before the legs fold in, Trina knows this is it. Algorithm is going to die. Here. Under her care. In the dressage ring of the university during the first week of holiday break.

II.

She is sitting on the ground in the dark with her back against the dead horse when Ender arrives. He switches on several additional banks of arena lights and enters, and she blinks up at him.

"Oh, my. He is really dead, isn't he?" Ender Chakrabarti stands with his hands in the pockets of his overcoat, a frail Indian man with an unevenly trimmed beard. Trina rents the cold water cabin on the east edge of Ender's land, walking distance from the school and her job at the experiment trailer in case her truck one of these days breaks down for good.

"Did you bring gloves?" Trina stands, her joints creaking. She is at least three inches taller than he, and thirty pounds heavier.

Ender shakes his head.

Trina speaks to the ceiling. "We're moving a dead animal and he doesn't wear gloves."

"George will have some," he says.

Trina has come to know the family not from renting their cabin, but from teaching their oldest daughter to ride. The vet school houses several donated riding horses, and some of the equestrian students are allowed to earn their semester's books by giving lessons to children on the weekends. Trina likes the girl well enough, but the Chakrabartis know nothing about ranching or horses. None of these people do, Trina thinks. The ones moving in, buying land. They mow the grass into straight grids of lawn and dig swimming pools. The Chakrabartis do not even own a dog.

"Can you tell me the history here?" He gestures toward the fallen horse. Ender is an anthropology professor. He asks questions like this.

"Dead," Trina says. "He has gone to meet his maker." She rubs warmth into her arms and jumps up and down a few times before standing still and turning toward the corridor to the trailer. "Listen. That'd probably be George, but let's get these lights off."

Trina stands with Ender at the front of the experiment trailer in the dark. Rows of bottles and stainless steel equipment wink in the lights of the truck as it approaches down the winding road.

"Why are we standing in the dark?"

Even over the sour smell of her own clothes and hair, Trina can smell Ender's delicate breath of spices and onions. Once a week she eats dinner at the Chakrabarti house after riding lessons. Their way of paying her, she supposes. The wife is American, but she cooks Indian food all day, chunks of chicken and lamb in sauces that she serves with rice and flat bread torn into little bits. Before this year, Trina has never had food like that anywhere.

"We don't know for sure that's George. It could be somebody else coming down here. Somebody who forgot something. Or those animal-politics crazy people."

"Tonight?"

"You never know."

Ender sighs and pulls his coat collar around his neck. "It's cold."

"Better safe than sorry. If it's George, we'll be working up a sweat here soon."

The headlights at last spear through the white andirons of the ag-school dairy and down the last rutted lane to the experiment trailer. The truck makes a heavy, diesel whine and drives too fast over the ditches, kicking up clouds of dust that refract its tail lights in a red glow.

"That's George," Trina says. "No doubt about it." She has seen this same huge truck approaching in just this way at the cabin. George serves as handy-man for several of the Chakrabartis' rental properties. He is exactly right for the job, Trina thinks. Repairs everything cosmetic with molly bolts and duct tape. Wears his pants low enough to show a crack when he works under a sink. Exactly the kind of repair guy landlords in college towns hire to keep costs down. But he is nice enough. Trina has several times sat on the front step of the Chakrabarti cabin drinking beer with George after he has finished cleaning the gutters or snaking out a pipe. He seems nice, and interested in her. He is really a mechanic, George has told her. The handy-man stuff is just a side line.

She flips the switches for the overhead lights, bringing on the fluorescents one after another in a receding row toward the arena.

They hear the engine cut and the door to the truck slam outside. Trina opens the door.

"You're going to need to back around to the arena side to load," she says, "but come on in for a minute and see what we're looking at."

A tall, thick man wearing coveralls and a fuzzy red hat enters and claps Ender on the back. "I didn't figure to find you around the animal torturers tonight of all nights. What's Jane and the kids doing?"

"She's watching something on television. The children are around."

"She know you're out here doing god knows what?"

"She was there when I took the call from Trina, yes. I told her it was one of Bhairavi's horses."

"It ain't?"

"It's an experiment horse," Trina answers. "They're not for riding. We had to say something."

The point none of them bothers to raise is the other option, that Ender might have stayed home by his fire with his wife. Perhaps it is the anthropologist in him, but Ender can never bring himself to miss a ritual event.

"I explained Trina's predicament. Another day of the year, the horse would simply be gone. We could say someone bought it. But, considering what night it is, I told Jane we would not want Bhairavi to go down to the school on Christmas morning and find one of the lesson horses dead. She understood this."

The men walk behind Trina toward the corridor. Ender holds his arms around himself for warmth. "What does one usually do in a situation like this?"

George shrugs. "I imagine they burn em up, don't they Trina? Incinerator?"

"Not something this large." She speaks over her shoulder. "We send them out. Dog food, whatever. You get about four hundred dollars for a healthy horse like this."

"Couldn't be that healthy. It's dead," George mutters.

They have stopped walking and stand at the entrance to the arena, looking at the dead horse lying nearly in the center.

"What about all the dissection horses?" George removes his hat and holds it in his hand.

Trina shoots him a menacing glance. "Those usually go out in smaller pieces along the way. Look, let's just get this going here."

The two men cross the quiet open space of the arena and stand looking down at the horse, which has fallen to one side. Arena peat clings to its hide and the blanket, still wet with sweat.

"It's quite a thing," Ender says.

"Yeah." George places his hat back on his head. "I guess I never thought much about what would happen in a case like this."

Trina calls to George from the doorway. "Look, I called Ender because he lives right north there, and he's the only person I know with any relation to a tow truck."

"What happens when Jane finds out it wasn't one of the school's riding horses at all, and we hauled one of these treadmill horses up and rolled it into your ravine? My sister ain't a force with which I plan to be reckoning in a case like that."

Ender shakes his head several times very slowly. "After the horse is buried, I do not imagine she will ever find out."

"What about the school? What are they gonna say?" George looks around uneasily. "I feel like we're committing a crime here. This can't be legal, taking State property."

Trina paces the distance between them and stands with her hands on her hips in front of George.

"I got a dead bleeder here in the middle of the dressage ring, and nobody coming back to work til January fifteenth. I can't authorize sending it out without a faculty signature. Now we can leave it here and hope like hell for cold weather the next few weeks, or we can get it the hell out of here."

"You got authorization to take it anywhere at all?"

"I'm in charge of what happens on this property until Dr. Breckmeier gets back from Spain. If he wants the horse back then, he can go dig it up."

"Do you think this is likely?" Ender pulls at his beard and cocks his head to one side.

"And have animal-rights people up here with a picket?" Trina turns and begins walking away from the two men. "I don't see that happening. This is the kind of thing the school tends to be subtle about."

"You have certainly thought this through thoroughly," Ender says.

Trina turns to George as she answers. "I'm in here with these animals every night. Alone. Don't think I haven't thought about the possibilities a long time before this."

"And my sister's ravine came right into your considerations." George spits to one side and stands squared to her.

"Look, if you don't want to help do it my way, you don't have to. Help me load it and we'll take it up to the dissection labs. If we can get a cart big enough, and there's room in the freezer, we can put it in cold storage."

George looks at Ender. "That sounds better to me. State property staying with the State."

Ender taps his fingers along the side of his face. This must be what he does when he is teaching, Trina thinks.

"Can you get to the lab without any trouble?" He cups his beard in his hand. All professors are the same, Trina thinks. Performers.

"Last time I went by there, there were about thirty or forty people in the picket."

"Yeah, I saw that on my way here." George shakes his head. "They're still out there, even tonight."

"Demonstrations have more punch on holidays," Trina says. "That's why they do it. Make the news. Peace on earth, good will to all living creatures."

The picket has been in front of the vet school sporadically for ten years, but since the treadmill accident with the girl from Lucas last year, it has grown constant. Protests have begun to peak around the holidays this year. The animal rights groups are demanding complete dissolution of the vet school donated animal projects and immediate cessation of experiments. So far they have not broken into the main building, but a number of donated greyhounds have gone missing, several doctors' houses have been vandalized, and one doctor's convertible was found turned completely upside-down and spray painted.

"I'm not driving my company truck through that loaded with a dead horse," George says.

"Well then, are you with this or not?" Trina looks pointedly at each man.

George shrugs. Ender nods his head.

The men follow her to a tack room off the arena floor, where she hands them each a coil of rope.

"We're going to tie that horse's legs together and then we're going to back George's truck in through the big doors over there as close as we can get it. We'll put George's tow line through the rope on the horse and use the winch to pull it up on to the platform. Then we'll just raise it up and drive it out of here."

"You ought to come work at the body shop with me," George says. He turns to Ender. "She sounds like she does this all the time."

They work in silence. Ender becomes less animated as the horse's legs are trussed. His eyes lack some of their usual brightness and interest, Trina thinks. The smile lines around them are gone. He looks tired.

"Not what you thought, eh?" The truck is backed through the arena loading doors now, and Trina shouts over the heavy rattle of the diesel engine. She makes a slip knot around the horse's four legs and pulls it tight, bringing the hooves together in a strange bouquet. "Just like the rodeo, except there you only have to do three."

Ender smiles only slightly. He shouts back, "How will you pull it now?"

She leans close and cups her hands around her mouth next to Ender's ear to be heard. "The winch will reel it in, just like you see on a wreck when they tow it off. We just pull it right onto that platform and then the platform raises up over the rear wheels."

George comes back from the cab of the truck and taps her on the shoulder. "You ready?"

Trina nods.

He walks back to the winch lever and stands facing the horse. Trina positions herself behind the horse's body on the dirt, checks the rope one more time, then signals George to begin winding in the spool of line.

It moves unevenly at first, the back-end and then the head. Trina follows in slow steps behind the body as it drags. There is a lip of metal where the platform meets the dirt unevenly. It is about the size of the space between the treadmill and the platform in the experiment trailer. The same danger of something moving meeting something still. The horse's legs are up at an angle, the winch pulling at about the height, Trina thinks, that a car bumper would be. They clear the platform easily, but the horse's ribs hit it with a heavy shudder. The animal's entire body shakes with the impact, but the winch hook does not come loose from the rope, and after a slight roll forward and back, the body begins sliding slowly up the incline of the platform.

She watches it onto the platform a few feet, then signals to George with one hand held flat in the air. Ender has turned the other direction, not looking. Trina thinks she knows how he feels. Something aches dully in her torso, as if it has been her own body pulled hard against the tow ramp. The school teaches students to turn off this empathy like a switch. The worst doctor, her professors tell her, is the one who stops for a crucial second because he's thinking about how it would feel. "These aren't your pets," they say. "We are professionals here." But here in the ring, outside the lab, it is hard for Trina to take her mind off the fact that they are loading something recently living, the horse whose sweat and hair still stain her clothing, whose blood waits in the vials of the experiment trailer.

Trina fastens her coat and pulls a hat from her pocket. "Let's go," she shouts to Ender. She pulls the hat over her head and bangs her gloved palms together.

Ender turns toward the truck and shakes his head. He moves close to Trina and leans in toward her to be heard over the engine. "I'm going back."

She raises her eyebrows at him in a question, and he answers her. "You have it now. I need to go back."

Trina nods and claps him on the shoulder. "Thanks for helping. It means a lot."

Ender walks rather stiffly toward George, to whom he says something before waving to Trina and walking out through the open doors of the ring into the night.

Trina climbs into the cab beside George. "He drive here?"

George nods. "His car's around front."

"Just great. I told him to park in back."

"We got just a small tarp over it." George punches the dashboard and heat begins flowing around Trina's legs and feet. Scraps of paper and cups litter the floor and swirl in the movement of air.

"We're going out the back. Chakrabartis' land goes right up to the vet school on the north side. We're not going to see anybody."

"You sure about that?"

"Well, that would be trespassing, plus what would be the point of a picket in the dark where nobody could see you?"

"True." George drops the truck into gear and looks over his shoulder one last time at the horse on the tow platform.

"I'll get out up here and pull the doors closed behind us," Trina says.

George nods. He drives slowly, staring toward the square of night sky framed in the open loading door of the arena.

III.

The tractor is a John Deere 46/40 with a front-end loader. Trina has run exactly this machine before, in another life before this one. The keys are just where she expects to find them, on a nail inside the Chakrabartis' machine shed. She has seen this tractor run once since renting the cabin, at harvest. They hire it done, she knows, they live in the house and hire out the land.

The horse scoops neatly into the loader, but is head hangs off limply, banging against rocks and undergrowth as the tractor rattles across the field. The sight of the horse, Algorithm, still in his blanket, damp as if sleeping in the loader, sends something fluttering in her chest. Trina feels something thrum and turn over in her. She looks away, out the window of the cab across the fields.

George is driving. The lights of the tractor spear ahead through a few new flurries, and he shouts over the rattle of the engine that the weather people are calling for more snow tonight. "Temperature's been dropping since afternoon. It was fifty-something when I took my dinner. Now look." He opens his mouth and exhales hard, forming a cloud.

The inside lights of the tractor reflect off the glass on all sides, sending images of Trina and George back to themselves, superimposed upon the dark fields.

"You want to start heading down that slope there, toward the ravine on the east side of the property," Trina shouts back.

"All right, but I'm taking it easy here. This thing ain't supposed to ride with the load up so high. I don't want to end up tumped over."

Trina watches as the tractor labors over a rut, lurches sickeningly to one side, then rights itself. The weight of the horse's head, hanging from one side of the loader, nearly pulls them over. In the headlights, Trina thinks she notices that the horse's ear is gone.

The ravine is more of a sinkhole filled with runoff that has been redirected as flood control from the dam which provides the massive new lake north of the city. Trina thinks of how an entire town lies flooded underneath this lake. Its streets and houses, trees and barns and deconsecrated cemeteries lie in a silent grid many feet below the glassy water. She has walked the dam and looked down, scanning the surface of the reservoir for some sign of this place, but there is none.

When they have reached the ravine, George lowers the scoop and cuts the engine of the John Deere. Working together, they unhook the safety chain and the horse comes heavily, rope and all, from the slant of the loader and down the embankment. In the deafening silence after the engine, they hear the weight of the animal meeting the water, then the sucking sounds of its body sinking beneath the sludge.

"Ain't frozen." George pulls off his gloves and lights a cigarette.

"Will be by morning, though."

He offers her a smoke but she refuses. "Suit yourself."

They stand in the empty night until their feet and faces numb with the cold. Trina thinks of the horse in his stall, nuzzling her chest after a run, eating a biscuit from her hand. The remembered warmth and size of the animal in close space resonates in her arms and chest. She has tried during these months to think of them all as the same horse: Algorithm, Blainey, Choctaw, Durango, and Easter. Five names derived from their experiment letters by the unfortunate treadmill jogger from Lucas. The stupid woman should not have named them, Trina thinks. And after she left, the school should have scratched the names off the stalls, leaving only the letters, A through E. Around Trina the night extends in snow hush, not even coyote or night bird to break the silence. There are four more horses, but this one is gone for good.

"Not what I thought I'd be doing tonight," George says.

"Me neither. I can't say I had any plans, though." Trina thinks of the remaining horses in their stalls. Two have been run already, the other two have not. They will be wild for movement by morning.

"Nope, I didn't either." George grinds his cigarette into the snow. "We should be getting back. Might be Jane has something up at the house to take the chill off."

Trina thinks of the experiment trailer and the locker room with the hot water shower. She will have to go back down to get her truck and clean up. The stables are warm enough, with the sleeping bag she keeps there. She can put up the folding cot in Algorithm's stall.

They climb back into the tractor and drive across the fields to the machine shed, then drive in George's tow truck toward the house. The snow whirls down harder now.

"Looks like it's coming north, then you turn west and it looks like it's coming west," he says. "Funny how that works, don't you think?"

He is trying, she knows. A big man in coveralls with nobody else to talk to this night. They have been through the secretive night burial of a once-living thing, and he wants it to mean something, but Trina can still smell the horse on her hands, in her hair. Algorithm. A stupid name for a horse. Trina leans her head against the cold glass of the truck window and watches the snow streaking toward the windshield. Her throat clenches hard, she feels heat and water brimming in her eyes, and she clears her throat.
"Yeah," she says. "It's weird."

"Ender wants us to stop up there and let him know things are okay." George turns the heat vent to defrost and rubs with a gloved hand at the windshield which is fogging from the bottom up, obscuring the snow.

"Better to hear about it than see it."

George laughs in a single bark. "Yep. I guess. Didn't take too well to seeing us load it, did he?"

"I'm surprised," Trina says. "Don't they travel all over the place, eating bugs with tribal people and monkeys and pig heads and stuff?"

"Maybe. I seen that on TV one time. People eating a monkey. They killed it right there and ate its brains right out of its head."

"I'm sure Ender would say that every culture has its barbaric tendencies."

"Yeah, I'm sure he'd say something like that." George exhales a long gust of air, then yawns. "How'd you know about their tractor and even know it had fuel in it?"

Trina sits up straight and smoothes her hat against her head.

"You been up there in that shed?" George does not look her way, but continues driving.

"I grew up on a farm," Trina says. "My mom was in the hospital most of her life. I worked alongside my dad since I was about ten, helping him do whatever needed done. That shed is exactly to the last nail the same as my father's machine shed back home where I grew up. Call it a good guess."

"Sorry. I didn't know. I never had any land. One of these days I'd like to. Working extra for Ender and Jane puts a little by. Might be I'll buy a piece of ground sometime here soon. Your old man raise stock or crops?"

"Both."

George sits silent for a moment. "He dead?"

"Yep." Trina pulls her gloves onto her hands again. The truck is turning onto the winding drive to the Chakrabarti house.

"A lot of people lost their land a few years back," George says. "I never was closer to it than the Farm Aid concert myself, but I knew people who lost everything. People I known since school having to move off to where there's work. Your family lose like that?"

"No. Not like that. But they lost it all the same."

"That's a hard thing." George cuts the engine in front of the house. The Chakrabartis' front door is covered in shiny foil paper and a bow to make it look like a giant gift. George turns to her with one arm over the back of the seat. "It sure seems to have made you tough, though."

Trina smiles for the first time this evening. "Yeah. Some things stick with you."

IV.

Over her protests the family has insisted that she come in, have something hot to drink, eat a cookie. They have built up the fire, before which bulging stockings hang. They celebrate Christmas, Trina thinks, and wonders if this is because of Jane. Ender is smiling now, animated. Jane, a heavy-set woman with blowsy hair wears a green and red jogging suit and thick slippers. She sets plates of fudge and cookies on the table and pours a spiced tea into tiny holiday mugs shaped like shoes.

"Quite a thing!" Ender rubs his wife's shoulders. "We have had an adventure tonight."

They all seem to have had nothing better to do this night, and in fact seem to be pleased for the diversion offered by the dead horse in the experiment trailer. Trina shakes her head. It is strange. The house and decorations are so new they do not look as if they belong to anyone in particular. Jane has placed blankets beneath Trina and George to protect the furniture. All around them, sheet rock and wall to wall carpeting. The massive holiday tree stands winking with lights in front of the large, south-facing windows that in daylight allow a view across the front sweep of field, Trina's own rented cabin, the vet school and the town beyond. She feels as if she is not here at all, but looking upward from her own window at the four people framed in this south-facing glass, all seated on mission wood furniture in front of a fire. It is a department store window. This is what is for sale.

Trina sips from the tea, and the sweet spice sets her stomach grumbling. She realizes she has not eaten and takes a cookie. It is warm and buttery. She takes another.

"I don't know how Bhairavi will take it," Jane says to Trina. "Maybe you can tell her the horse was bought by someone."

Trina nods.

"I'm so glad you all took care of it tonight, though. She might have wanted to ride tomorrow. It could have really ruined things."

Trina does not bother to point out that the school, like everything else, will be closed tomorrow. Even people like Trina will have the day off, whether the girl wants to ride or not. It is better that Jane see it this way. Jane is like everyone around here. She sees things the way she wants them to be.

"Well it's all water under the bridge now." George takes a piece of fudge. His face is warming, reddening from the ears inward. Trina notices that in this light he is almost handsome, the shadow of stubble at his jaw, the graying temples. He is a hefty and not-very-handy repairman. She is tall, big-framed, going soft in the chin, and forty-three. The next oldest student in the vet school is thirty-two. Trina sighs and eats another cookie. She is thickening in the hips, flat in the chest. Crow's feet around the eyes and deep frown lines on either side of her mouth. Forty-three. Who is she to judge? She feels the tea working, the warmth coming again to her hands and feet.

Jane tops her tea again. "We have been just so lucky to have you living in the cabin this year, working with Bhairavi and all. Tell George how you came to be in vet school now, Trina."

Trina stops chewing a bite of cookie. George is nodding. Ender has wrapped himself in a housecoat and is smiling at her from his chair.

She thinks of George in the arena, squared against her. In her ears, Trina still hears the roar of the horse's running, echoing from the steel walls of the trailer. She feels the forward strain of the horse in the bridle, the hot fog of its body steam in the cold experiment room.

"We're not just hacking them up down there. We're trying to understand. I didn't breed them like this. I didn't name them or race them. I'm the one who comes after. I give them their fix. I run them until they can't run anymore."

"She wants to be a veterinarian. She wants to be a healer." Ender reaches for Trina's hand and holds it in his own. His hands are soft as cat fur, she thinks. Her own hands are calloused and thick-fingered, the nails flayed into mica from scrubbing and solvents.

"She wishes to improve the condition of living things." He gives her hand a squeeze, a gesture so overly sentimental and strange she cannot react. She feels the long, straight bones of Ender's hands like the ribs of an umbrella under his smooth skin. She cannot remember the last time another person has held her hand for any length of time.

Jane smiles. There has been entirely too much smiling. For a moment, Trina suspects they are about to tell her about a religion that has changed their lives, but Ender takes his hand away, reaches for a square of fudge, and asks her to continue.

"Where do you expect to practice, once you finish your degree?"

Trina wonders whether they are thinking about her age, or about the horse that has died this night under her care.

"I don't know. I guess I haven't thought that far ahead. I had some money from my mother's estate. Her lawyers sold quite a bit of land and equipment awhile back. I wanted to start something new. This is what I wanted to do. Understand how animals work. I wanted to come back here."

"Me too," George says. "I was living up in Kearney. Working. Not very happy. Marriage busted up. I came back and got on at the garage and started doing some work for Jane and Ender. Just wanted to be back to home."

"When did you come back, Trina?" Jane leans her head almost flirtatiously on her hand, her elbow propped on the arm of the chair.

They must be trying to fix her up with George, Trina thinks. This night has been part of a dating mechanism. Ender must be studying them: mating rituals of mid-life, mid-western singles. The next question will be whether she is or has ever been married.

"It's all changed since I knew this area." She shakes her head. "My husband left me in '90 and married a kid who worked for him at the plastics plant in Evanston. We moved up there from here. He ran the small assemblies line. They made windshield scrapers and travel mugs. Every time it snows, I think of that place." Trina wraps her arms around herself. "The girl was eighteen and already pregnant when they got married."

Jane shakes her head. "What a jackass. No offense meant."

"None taken. Winters have been warming in Evanston the past so many years anyway. No future in it." Trina grins. "I shouldn't ever have married him in the first place, but I finished undergrad and was trying to start a master's in biology. He was the first one to come along and take me away from my father's house. You know how that can be. My dad died before they built the dam. My mom just passed a couple years ago. Before I came back this last year, I hadn't been back here since dad died."

"It is interesting you mention the dam. This entire area was once a flood plain." Ender gestures with one hand at the large south window.

"Did you have any brothers and sisters, Trina?" Jane asks.

"One. A sister. She died really young. Nine years old. My mom never really got over it."

Jane makes a tisk sound and shakes her head. "I'm sorry. Such a terrible, terrible shame. We never expect to outlive our children."

Ender continues as if he has not been interrupted. "All the great cities have been the result of man's ability to conquer nature to some degree and claim land. Flood plains are extremely rich agriculturally, but unstable. The cradle of civilization is the flood plain. The Aswan Dam in Egypt, case in point, demonstrates how this land can be stabilized."

The same tilt of the head, the hand tugging at the beard. Trina wonders whether Ender practices these movements as part of his lectures, or if they come naturally.

"Oh, Ender." Jane rolls her eyes.

George stretches his arms above his head and shakes himself awake. "Getting too settled here in front of this fire." He raises his eyebrows at Trina.

"You see? You've started lecturing these people right out into the snow." Jane swats Ender playfully.

"No offense." George stands and hugs his sister with one arm. "It's been a longer day than I planned."

Trina stands too. George asks her if she wants a ride back down, and she says she does. Jane frets over a tray of food, wrapping it in plastic and insisting that they take some with them. Trina and George bundle into their coats and boots again. They stand at the door, George holding two plates of food, Trina with her hands in her pockets, and the Chakrabartis with their arms around each other's waists.

"Thanks again," Trina says to Ender. "And you too, George. You got me out of a tough spot. You really didn't have to do it, either."

"I'm happy to be of service," Ender replies.

"Sorry this happened tonight," Jane says.

"Happy Christmas," Ender says.

"Merry Christmas," George and Trina answer together.

"We'll expect you for dinner tomorrow, George. And you too, Trina," Jane says. "You're welcome to come on up too, if you like."

Outside the snow is thicker, covering the cobbled path from the house to the truck, and they step slowly, measuring their balance. The sound of their movement is swallowed in the hush of weather.

"Listen." Trina stops on the driveway and pulls her hat from her head.

"What?" George stands still and cocks his head to one side. "I don't hear anything."

"Exactly."

Below them the lights of the town are a smudged halo on the horizon, muted by the swirling snow. Trina thinks of the horse as it must be by this time, submerged in the gelid sludge, slowly freezing. Its stall empty now. A is for Algorithm.

"None of this used to be here," she says as they climb into the big truck again and begin the drive down the long hill toward the lights.

"Probably all farmland," George says. His breath fogs the windshield more quickly than the defroster can clear it, and he leans forward over the steering wheel to see out through a narrow clear space near the dash.

"They bulldozed all the houses and fences under the ground and under the lake. It's all still there underneath."

The truck reaches the gate at the end of the Chakrabarti drive and turns southward onto the rutted road that leads to the vet stables.

Trina places her hand on George's arm. "Stop the truck." She rolls down the window and looks out at a clot of scrub trees slowly dissolving in the snow next to the machine shed.

"This was our house."

"Their shed?"

"No. The shed is the same. The cabin was the milk barn then." Trina feels large wet flakes of snow against her cheeks as she stares out the open window. It will be a white Christmas, as the song says.

"My dad worked the farm until he dropped dead of a heart attack. He was fifty-two. My sister drowned when she was nine. And my mom lived in the hospital most of her life. She never really came back to us after that. She died two years ago. Now they're all gone."

Trina opens the door of the truck and steps out into the snow. In the shadow of the thicket, the road is dark, overhung by a gray sky of refracted light. She hears George cut the engine, his door open and shut, his footsteps coming around to her side of the truck. He places one arm around her. She cannot feel anything through her coat but his presence, large beside her.

"It's easy to get lonely around the holidays." His voice is hushed and thick in the falling snow.

Trina turns to view the house on the hill, its Christmas tree lit in the front window, the yellow light of a fire flickering behind it. It has grown late. The protesters will all be gone now, home with their families. The vet school will be empty and dark. Animals will be curled in their stalls, deep in the straw. Or frozen. Some of them are frozen. It is called plasticizing, the injection of liquid plastic into the aorta. The animals die in their sleep, their flesh slowly hardening. This is how the students study the circulatory systems and musculature. The flesh is no longer flesh, but something hard that peels and splits into fibrous strata. Breckmeier's new area of study will be to plasticize the bleeders after they die in order for future veterinary students to understand what happens when this generation of animals lives past maturity. There is a whole process involved. Trina has rehearsed it many times in the lab, injecting mice in order to know, when the time comes, how to preserve each horse.

In front of Trina the Christmas tree lights suddenly blink off, and the window on the hill is an empty square of flickering light. There are still four more horses, she thinks. B through E will be examined and understood by subsequent classes of students. Only A will remain a mystery. The horse belongs to this place, now. To her.

George moves between her and the view of the house. The conical shape of his hat obscures the window and the driveway. He pulls off his gloves and drops them, then places his hands on either side of Trina's head. She realizes her hair is wet already with the falling snow. Her eyelashes are sticking with it. When he kisses her, a big man in coveralls and a funny hat, it is not as she would have expected it at all. His mouth smells of the tea and fudge they have eaten, and his lips are very warm. The same tug comes in her chest that she felt earlier in the tractor.

"Don't be sad," he says.

"I'm not sad." She holds her gloved hands to his. "You don't understand." For a moment the solid shape of the man in front of her brings back the remembered movement of the horse, the rhythm of its running beside her and the pulse of its life under her hands. She lifts her face to the snow.

"I lived here. In the house buried under that one."

His wide hands smooth her ears and neck. "It's all right." George pulls her to him and rocks slightly back and forth. They stand in the falling snow under the silent sky. "It's that time of year. Makes things hard to let go. Lot a family stuff. The horse stuff. You gotta let it go. Save your own life."

"You're right." Trina turns her head to one side, resting her cheek against George's coat, which smells, like her own father's coat, of automotive oil and cigarettes. The door of the truck is still open on her side, and she watches the outline of the window dissolving in the whirling snow. She smiles. "Yes. It was a hundred years ago. Before the human beings we know were even formed."

Prairie Paradox

—for P.J.

On the eve of your farewell I cast into this gold
slanting light, melancholy with knowing
this special June of rain on the roof,
fields green without end, and yellow
tufted wheat that is lifting with rising wind
will be your last season here.

Axiomatic, how the coming of grief is certain
but never without a gift in its hands,
how your leaving offers some lesson
I will keep, though it seems impossible
this fecund July we will lie on our backs
hands starring the air, wet
with the juice of beefsteak tomatoes
we have plucked swollen from the vines,
warm as hearts. We will hear the descant
of frogs thrumming these nights of stars,
the snap of dragonflies at the screen, and know
you are gone from this place.

Surely what matters is not the rending of the seam,
but the way I tear the hem of this skirt to run
this length of pasture, dogs alongside,
not the door closing warm kitchen light
behind me, but the field of fireflies
winking this new dark.

This quiet moment I am thinking of you
as the horizon blues, auguring signs.
A dart of starlings opens the sky and I feel
the paradox, the absence
your presence has brought—

       Not the coming of change,
       but our witness to its passing.
       Not the flight of birds,
       but the music they whistle.

II.

Love keeps us together
And love will drive us insane
And we are criminals who never
Broke no laws
All we needed was a net
To break our fall

—Talking Heads, "Sax and Violins" (1988)

Helping

It is not the drunken leaning of the row houses into one another for mile upon gray mile. The skim-milk morning sky. The lead-sinking clouds of exhaust, or the cars, everywhere rusting, patched, missing bumpers or upturned, stripped to the frames. It is not even the claustrophobic encroachment of it all, the people, the machines, the way the rotted and peeling wooden houses line the roads like teeth clamping in. It is the voice.

Crick's has become the voice Brosius hears when he is driving the freeway each day to the warehouse from the house where his wife sits waiting for him to make another mistake. You sonofabitch. Fuck around on my sister. Fucking kill my sister with your fucking around. I oughtta fucking kill you. Crick's words, in any combination, the same rosary, Brosius at one end, strung with these two verbs to his wife at the other.

It is nearly six months ago now that Crick, with his large fist curled around a cup of Brosius's wife's coffee, sat at the table in Brosius's kitchen telling him that he, Brosius, could work in the family building supply yard or the warehouse, either one, so long as he, Crick, did not have to see him.

"She's better off with her mother and me." Brosius's wife's brother sighed and tipped the last gulp of coffee from the cup. Crick is a large man, not tall, but thick through the neck and torso. On that day, he leaned across the table at Brosius and said, "I know it sucks hearing it, but it's true. Why are you still fucking around trying to take care of her? She needs someone who can provide for her. You got no plan, no decent job, no skills, no nothing." Crick's outstretched arm implied the tiny apartment, the sagging furniture, Brosius's wife sleeping in the other room. "You're still in a dump."

Brosius stared at the other man. He was outweighed by, he estimated, sixty pounds easily. The last time he had been in a fight he had been in high school, an argument about a girl. His opponent had broken his nose. Brosius looked directly into the eyes of the man across from him.

"I appreciate your help and your concern. But you're her brother," Brosius said. "She's my wife. I want to do it my way."

The way emotion came upon Crick, Brosius noticed as if it were happening on film, was that the blood flooded in first, reddening his ears and face, and then he began, inadvertently or on purpose, Brosius could not have said, to clench and unclench his hands into fists. In front of Brosius, Crick seemed to grow larger and begin to emanate something, power or violence, if those things were different. He was not a person, Brosius imagined, who was accustomed to being refused. Crick stood and bent forward so that his face was close enough to Brosius's that Brosius could feel the heat of his skin.

"You can start tomorrow, but I don't know you. I don't want to see you. I don't want to hear word one about you. The only reason I want you there at all is to make sure you got a steady check to bring home to my sister. It's not about you at all."

Crick rose from the table then, carried his cup to the sink and rinsed it. Brosius dug his toes hard into the linoleum deeply scarred by countless tenants in what he imagined alternatively as more or less desperate straits than his own. Imagined the cup shattering in Crick's hand. Tried to summon rage, rage being easier than what he felt instead. Failed. He had been without work for five weeks. Brosius went to work at the building supply yard the next day. What could he do?

Brosius totes and tallies stock in the brother's warehouse. He worked, first, the nights because Crick drove Brosius's wife to her mother's house nights. On the late shift, he had worked with Dardin, who confided during Brosius's first week that his wife was planning to spend the weekend in New York State with some friends she had met on the internet.

"What kind of friends does she think she's going up there for?" Dardin paced while Brosius pulled machine parts for a building order. A week later, Dardin wiped tears from the corners of his eyes with a handkerchief. "She says she's leaving me. For some guy she met up there. She's not taking the kids, and they're her kids. Only the boy's mine."

Brosius listened every night. Sometimes he wondered what Dardin might have been like before the internet man, before Brosius met him. Not much different, he thought. Quieter maybe.

And then Brosius's wife wanted him to work days. "Normal" hours. A normal life. Crick glowered at Brosius in the break room, waving a blue slip. "You better be home with her every night."

Less than a full shift later, Menendez began riding him. "Who'd you suck, man?" The little man appeared behind him in the warehouse on Brosius's last Friday of night shift.

"What are you talking about?" Brosius stopped, mid-count in a box of plastic pipe.

"Blue slip. I seen you got a blue slip. You work up to day shift faster than anybody I ever seen, man." Menendez, leering, flipped a cigarette still lit under the steel shelves of parts. "You gotta blow somebody around here to work onto days so fast."

"I wouldn't know anything about that." Brosius began counting again, from the beginning. That was when Dardin came back with coffee.

"He giving you shit, Mikey?" Dardin handed Brosius one Styrofoam cup and peeled the lid back from the other. To Menendez he whispered, "You better be careful what you say to this one. He'll end up your boss."

"Knock it off, Dardin." Brosius started to explain. He had worked through a story in his mind about the blue slip—I have a family situation. I need days. It's not personal. He looked at Dardin's face and thought better of saying it.

"What you patting him on the back all the time for?" Menendez turned to Dardin. "He be too good for us once he gets onto days anyhow."

Menendez stalked away, digging with a toothpick at his front teeth, which had recently been loosened when Menendez had taken a hit full in the mouth by a pipe fitting bounced from a truck on the loading dock.

Dardin stared at Brosius. "He's just pissed off. Don't take it personal." Dardin pushed his safety glasses tighter against his rabbit-face. Rabbit teeth, rabbit cheeks, Dardin had everything but the ears, Brosius thought. He would not be sorry to get away from Dardin's nightly litanies. Still, he felt something of a betrayal in this movement from third shift to first. How long had Dardin been waiting for a promotion to day shift while his wife stared at the computer screen, night after night?

Dardin continued bitterly, his eyebrows raised above the flat black line of his safety glasses. "You know what I mean? Crick goes and takes an interest in you, it makes sense. You work. Menendez don't work. He ain't going to be like you. You can't take it personal."

Brosius shook his head. He sipped the coffee through a tear in the plastic lid and felt it burn the skin of his tongue and the roof of his mouth just behind the teeth.

"Thanks, man." He extended a weak punch toward Dardin's arm, but Dardin was already moving away, nodding as he pulled his clipboard from one of the shelves and shuffled down the cavernous aisle of dark bins.

As of today, Brosius will have been on day shift for eight weeks. The voice is somehow stronger now, with each day he drives into rather than away from the industrial district with dawn approaching. Fucking kill you.

His wife, waiting. Brosius works. It is a contribution he can measure in the aching bones of his back, the metal-knicked and bloody joints of his fingers.

The truth was that back then, in Phoenix, in the life that had been their life before this, Brosius had failed her. Whether his fault lay in having caused her pains or having failed to alleviate them, Brosius could not have said, but when they had wrung themselves out with yelling and crying and staring at one another, she had, finally, asked to go home. Brosius had said yes. What could he say? It was important to be near people who loved you, who could help you. He knew something of what it would mean. The siphoning into plastic partitioned boxes the dosages of pills. The mind-numbing acronyms and account numbers affixed to terrifying balances on insurance and billing paperwork. The silence of waiting with her under the same buzzing fluorescent strip light into which ten, twenty, maybe a hundred different clinicians would come with more complicated and confusing news. He knew it was serious, and Brosius knew he would stay. He promised. He begged. He ranted from the outsides of locked bathroom doors.

But when the distrust worked in his wife like a corrosive, there was nothing more for it but to sell one car and hitch the other to a rented truck heaped with everything else, and drive himself, his wife and their life to Kansas, a state to which he had never been. Brosius does not remember the trip. He remembers his wife asleep in the dark seat across him through the night. She woke in the washed morning light of New Mexico with a pink stripe down her cheek and two semi-circular indentations from the buttons of a wadded shirt she had stuffed between her head and the window.

"I love you," he said to the side of her head. Nothing in the ribbon of straight road and scrub land in front of them on which to keep his eyes. He stared full across the cab at the profile of her face. She took a brush from her bag and began to pull it slowly through the snarls of her hair. Nothing but the whitening light. We may come to harm, he thought. We may come to mend.

It is Friday. Menendez has plans for the fight, and he's working the line too fast. At the bottom, Brosius stands with the kid, Jimmy Finney, pulling roofing tiles as they come shuddering down the ramp of heavy metal rollers. The air is cool enough now in the mornings that they can see their breath. In the quiet of the yard, it is all the two at the bottom can do to heave the tiles from the line and onto the flats before Menendez levers another load toward them with his long metal pole.

Only eight weeks, and already it feels like eight years, day shift being no better than night except in being lighter. There is something worse, Brosius thinks, in being able to see it all come into relief against the gray morning sky—the building supply yard, the yawning warehouse doors, and the trucks, waiting, laden with freight that people like Dardin will sort into bins throughout the night.

"Hey, hold it up there!" he shouts to Menendez at the top of the ramp.

"You speed up, boys," he speaks to Brosius, below him in the yard. "I'm ready to punch out. You got two of you day-boys down there, and I'm way ahead of you working all by myself." He grins, revealing the space of missing front teeth. "I can't stick around and do your shift for you. I got to drive all the way out and pick up my cousin today, man, then try an' get some sleep before tonight. Help me out here."

The kid laughs stupidly, slinging another row of tile on top of the last.

"Not so hard. You crack it and they'll take it out of your pay," Brosius says, but the kid just hurls the tiles as quickly as Menendez can lever them down the squealing and rattling ramp. Menendez and the kid smile at each other, working faster, as if they are in a race. Brosius pulls another tile and stacks it evenly across the top of the flat. It is different for them, he knows. It is just a job. It is not about the same things at all.

When tiles surround him on all sides, Brosius waves both arms over his head, gesturing over the noise to Menendez to stop the line. The kid stops first, turned half away from the rollers with a tile in his hand as another tile, sent down by Menendez, falls to the ground and cracks in half.

"We're full up. Lay off a minute."

Brosius does not wait for Menendez to answer, but climbs into the forklift and starts the engine. He picks up the closest flat of tiles and drives it over to the fence on the far side of the building. It looks lonely, he thinks when he leaves it, one orange-red cube of tile, waiting by itself. By the end of the week there will be flats of tile stacked along the entire length of the fence for summer building on Elsinore Ridge, an encampment of upscale homes overlooking Kansas City and the surrounding litterlike sprawl of apartment houses like his own.

When he returns to the warehouse conveyor line, Brosius sees that Menendez has swung his legs over the railing and is talking to the kid, who is working one of the rollers one direction with his right hand, and the other the opposite direction with his left. He looks to Brosius like a scrawny bird flapping its wings.

Brosius cannot hear them, but he sees Menendez nod. Sees him laugh.

As he works the tines of the forklift under another flat, Brosius watches the kid pick up the broken tile from the ground and hold it over the spinning rollers. Brosius slams his hand to the steering wheel of the forklift, as if this is traffic, as if at somebody recklessly merging into his lane on I-435. But there is no horn, only the laboring rattle of the forklift engine. Even at this distance, Brosius can see the nervous excitement etched in the kid's face. He is not even wearing safety glasses. Brosius watches the kid drop the tile onto the spinning rollers and it explodes in a spray of orange-red pieces. Menendez, hanging out of the open warehouse tier above, ducks the shrapnel.

Brosius clamps his teeth together hard and wheels the second flat of tiles away toward the fence. By the time he has driven six flats of tile to the fence, Menendez is standing in the yard with his arms crossed over his chest, waiting.

"I'm clocking out, man." Menendez scowls at the lightened sky as though it has made an obscene gesture to him. "Probably seven-thirty by now. I'm way into OT."

Brosius simply nods. He looks toward the flats stacked alongside the building, a small and lonely row of the massive wall of new freight for the Elsinore project. "Go ahead."

In front of him, lip twisting in the space of now-absent teeth, Menendez looks to Brosius like that boxer. Not the religious one Menendez likes, but the other one, the macho. Menendez should put his money on the other guy, Brosius thinks. The clean-cut boy is going to get killed. Brosius could watch that fight himself at the bar tonight, if his wife falls asleep early, if she has taken all the pills instead of hiding them in the dresser drawer, the folds of the pillowcase. Brosius has felt these pebbles under sofa cushions, seen them spill from wadded filters full of coffee grounds in the trash. This is why he knows, even though it would be possible, he will not go to the bar, not see the fight. His wife can find too many places for hiding.

When Menendez quick-steps away out of the yard toward the locker room, Brosius turns again to the line. He and the kid will not finish it today, no matter who Crick gets to pole the loads down. But Crick will pick the worst, the slowest and stupidest, to stand above him all day. Brosius knows by the curt nods in the locker room, the brusque retreats into the paneled office from any chance encounter at vending machines or drinking fountain. The sight of him sickens Crick with rage. Brosius feels it like a metal plate against him, an enduring kind of rage.

The fact that Brosius's wife was going to be sick anyway was not what mattered. Brosius could see this from Crick's point of view. Simply, if Brosius had been more stable, a better provider, home more. If he had lived closer to his wife's family from the start instead of estranged and family-less himself. If he had earned more and carried better insurance they might have taken her conditions more seriously and sought treatments earlier. If he had been altogether more unlike himself and more like Crick, perhaps he would have given her less worry and fewer reasons to fret and become confused. Simply, if Brosius had been different from who he was, perhaps his wife would not have ended up breaking down so fast.

More importantly, if Brosius would just go away his wife would be amply provided for. He was the outsider. He stood in the way of everything his wife's mother and brother could do for her. And why? Brosius could see the way Crick sneered at him as if challenging: What kind of man did Brosius think he was?

And maybe some of it was true.

Brosius has plenty of time to work it one way and other while he stacks and tallies and lifts and heaves through stock. He could have been home. He could have taken less pleasure in hurting back when she hurt him first, before he knew. When she accused him of things she accused him of, he could have stopped himself before he said things he'd said, things that could not be taken back and that made her worse. But he hadn't known. And what the voice suggests to him is that it should not have made any difference whether he knew or not, whether she could take it or not. Even if she had been well, she should not have had to take it.

It is harm. It can heal.

It would be easier by far to leave. But there are times when the fear and confusion subside and for a short time she is there with him. This woman whom he first loved is a woman who would have said to someone like Crick, "It's our life. Butt the hell out."

Beside him in the yard, the kid has lit a cigarette and stands rigidly, blowing smoke in a hard, straight line toward his feet.

"Less go." He rocks back and forth, heel and toe. Plows the long white fingers of one hand through his greasy black hair.

"We got to wait until Crick gets somebody up top."

"You an' me can do it. You go up and I'll stack." The kid gestures expansively at the lot behind him. "We can finish this up in, maybe, two tens. Get Sunday and Monday off."

"It doesn't work that way," Brosius answers. "You have to work four tens and then you get Friday through Sunday. And that's only assembly and sales." It is another piece of the knowledge, large and small, that he has archived since leaving Arizona—four weeks to forklift licensing. A dozen pipe fittings to a short box, sixty-four to a long. Fifteen liquor stores and twelve churches between his street and Crick Building Supply. His wife has taken seventeen different combinations of doses of medication. The medical insurance provided by the building supply job covers exactly two-thirds of the costs of these medications.

"Shit." The kid shoves his long bare white hands into his jacket pockets. "They should let you add up your hours any way they add up. Who you got to be related to around here to get onto A and S?"

"Couldn't tell you." Brosius pulls a lace tighter on one boot and produces a towel from the seat of the forklift. "There's some oil in the box by the freight door. Go and get it and rub some of those drums so they don't squeal so bad. I'll see who's gonna work the top."

"Can you get me a Dr. Pepper? I forgot any change."

Brosius nods, walking away. The kid, standing in the blank morning light. About one-ten soaking wet. Every day, a snack cake and soda from the machine, swallowed haltingly at the break table. The kid is wasting away to nothing. Where does his money go? Brosius thinks of himself, pulling on socks his wife has washed and folded. It makes her feel good, feel useful. Who washes that kid, Finney's socks?

At the office, Brosius finds that Crick has gone out. He stands outside the paneled door, looking at the pushpin in the OUT column. No estimated time of return has been chalked in. When a secretary tells Brosius Crick has gone to Receiving, he follows her gesturing arm to the first tier of the warehouse where three men stand shiftlessly, watching a tow truck back toward the ramp. Brosius follows one of the men's suggestion to look for Crick in the break room, then another suggestion from someone in the break room to look for Crick in Lumber. Passing the office again, Brosius sees again the pushpin: OUT. He thinks of the line of red cubes in the yard, the wall of red tile in the upper tier. Brosius resolves to find someone in Lumber to pile the tiles down. There are always guys standing around in Lumber. He is walking toward the lumber section, past the locker room along the back east wall. The boys from Lumber are moving past him in a line, their gloves stained with brown sap and the red of maple flesh. Brosius sees, startlingly, that everyone is moving past him, even Menendez, now in jeans and a jacket, his hair slicked with water and his uniform rolled under one arm.

"—always was a little slow," Brosius hears one of the lumber boys say, moving past him toward the yard.

"Boy couldn't tell the difference tween a skunk and a skateboard."

It is only these pieces of conversation and the general movement of men toward the yard, but Brosius knows in this moment. He knows as if he has seen it happen.

It is a trucker from WestFreight who, the buzz through the crowd informs Brosius, saw him and pulled him out. Brosius can see, behind the clutch of men standing around the roller line, the blue and white WestFreight truck, driver's side door open, parked and idling, a forty-five degree angle between cab and trailer, as though the driver had been pulled suddenly from the seat in mid-turn by a giant vaudevillian hook. Brosius knows but does not want to swallow the copper taste of knowing. A Shirt from A and S directs the trucker past Brosius and toward the office.

The trucker stutters uncontrollably. "I swear, I just drove in here and saw him."

The ambulance comes, as clean and efficient as television. Even after they have taken the boy away, have wrapped the arm and placed it beside him on the stretcher, the men remain, stunned, staring at the empty gate through which the ambulance has gone and the truck remains, half turned, still idling. Someone pulls a lumber tarp over the slicked and garish rollers.

The supervisor from Parts lights a cigarette and turns to Brosius. "Nineteen years old. Jesus." He blows the smoke out hard, in a straight line that makes Brosius turn away.

Two men from Lumber turn with him. "Wasn't nobody could have saved him," one says. Under their boot soles, splinters of red tile crunch like new snow.

He should have been there, he knows. Once again, he has been in the wrong place, doing the wrong thing, been the wrong person entirely. Now the first thing Brosius faces when he appears in the middle of the morning is his wife's concern that Crick has fired him. She is sitting on the couch, surrounded by balls of yarn and covered to the waist in a half-woven blanket pierced with pins.

"Oh my god. What did you do?"

Brosius unlaces his boots before stepping onto the carpet, and stands there with them slung from his hand like two shot birds.

"I didn't do anything. There was an accident." He walks past her into the bedroom and she follows.

"Were you responsible? What happened?"

Brosius sags to the bed and looks at her, draped in the doorframe.

She is still pretty. She will always be pretty. He tries to summon other feelings, angry words in his own defense, but cannot. He pats the mattress beside him, motioning her to sit down.

"Mike. What happened?"

"I'm tired, Angie." Brosius rolls toward her and buries his face into the side of her leg. She smells of yarn. "I mean it."

"Are you going to tell me what happened or do I have to call Bobby to find out?"

"Crick wasn't even there." Brosius rolls away from her and folds his arms beneath his head. "I went looking for him and nobody could find him. When I got back this kid, Jimmy Finney, had got his arm pulled into a roller ramp. Somebody tried calling Crick when they took him away in the ambulance, but I don't know if anybody found him."

"My god. Was the kid all right?"

Brosius swallows hard and screws his eyes tight against the vision of the kid. Brosius can see him in the yard, waiting, pacing. Brosius sees him oiling the roller bars with the rag. Sees the thin white fingers working down one drum and up the next. Sees the moment when the kid stands back, glances furtively over his shoulder toward the warehouse, then leans in with one hand on one roller and one hand on another. It probably happens at the moment when the kid holds the broken tile above the rollers. Perhaps the towel dangles loose from the end of the kid's jacket sleeve, or perhaps the kid still clutches the towel beneath the tile as he drops it, and the split-second instinct to fetch it pulls him in after the white scrap of cloth.

Brosius cannot stop seeing it one way and the other, each leading to the moment of the men standing, blank and amazed, the slick rollers and the red-soaked rag, midpoint in a circle of sharp red shards.

"What do you think? Of course he was not all right." She winces back, and he is sorry but cannot stop himself. "I've never seen so much blood in my life. They—"

"That's enough!" She stands alongside the bed staring down at him. "I don't want to hear the gory details."

"Really?" Brosius can feel it now. It is a thing he cannot stop, even though he knows he will be sorry later. "I thought you wanted to know all about it. Would that make everything seem more real to you?" He rises from the bed and follows her as she backs from the room. "Would it give you something to worry about besides how you're going to drag yourself through another day?"

She is crying. The way he knows. Brosius pulls her to him but she pushes him away, hands tight against her face. She speaks to him facing the wall.

"Get out of here."

"I'm sorry, Angie. I swear to god, I'm just worn out. It's wearing me thin, honey. I swear. If you could have seen this kid, I mean—"

She lets out a keening wail, cutting him off, and when he tries to pull her to him she goes rigid as a bat. Brosius crosses the room to the cluttered kitchen whose window faces another row of houses just like this one, each divided into apartments just like this one. He dials the mother and tells her to come over. Something has happened. Then his wife is standing in front of him, swollen-eyed, fierce and hurt.

"If you leave here, you might as well not come back."

"Angie honey, I'm gonna let you talk with your mom a while. I'll be back later."

"You won't."

"I will. You just said you wanted me to go away for a while. But I'm coming back."

"I don't believe you."

"You have to believe me, honey. I'm coming right back. I'm gonna stay with you until your mom comes over, and then I'm going out for a while. But then I'm coming right back."

He reaches to touch her cheek, wiping at the wetness there. The vulnerability seeps from her face like water drawn into sand. Brosius watches the sneer emerge to replace it, a bitter mouth-twist that transforms his wife into this person who jerks her head back from his touch. Brosius has tried to hate this person as something separate from his wife. He has failed.

"You better be walking in here by six o'clock or I start throwing your stuff out into the street. That's all I got to say." She turns unsteadily on one heel and stalks away from him into the bathroom. Brosius hears the lock click into place.

Two hours before dinnertime, Brosius is sitting in a bar off of I-435. The whoosh of traffic in the distance sounds like an ocean swelling against the walls of the bar. A few exits up is the building supply yard. A series of interchanges away is his wife, who will be waiting for him at six o'clock. Brosius orders a beer.

The surprising thing is that, as Brosius slouches over the frosted bottle, Dardin walks in. He still wears his uniform, safety glasses bulging from the chest pocket. Dardin sees Brosius immediately. There is no one else in the bar.

"Mikey! Hey, what are you doin' here?"

"Same as you, I guess, but I don't know. Four o'clock, man. You not on night shift anymore? Why aren't you working?"

"Aw, man. They shut down the whole yard until OSHA can come out and check the site where that Finney kid got mangled up today."

"Crick ever show up?"

Dardin looks at him curiously, and orders a beer.

"He showed up all right. Pretty pissed off at you, word goes."

"At me?"

"Word is you was supposed to be watching that kid when he got pulled in. Said you left him down there to pull tiles by himself."

"We weren't even working. There wasn't even anybody up top. Menendez said he wanted overtime and then flaked. As a matter of fact, that's when I left him, was to go find Crick and get things moving."

Dardin holds his glass at an angle as he pours from the bottle. He does not look at Brosius. "Well, you know how people get a story going, Mikey. It's nothing personal." Dardin glances at Brosius quickly, over his shoulder. "You talk to OSHA, it'll all get straightened out. Everybody will know everything."

Brosius rubs his temples with his fingers. He can see Menendez in front of him in the yard as the ambulance pulled away, arms crossed over chest and glowering. Himself and Menendez, locked in a challenging stare: You're the one who taught him the stupid trick and You're the one who was supposed to be watching him. Brosius can see, again, the hard glimmer in Menendez's eyes as he turned away. Can see himself walking straight to his car and driving home. He remembers now that he did not clock out.

"Oh, hell, Dardin." Brosius sighs. "It's a bad scene."

Dardin brightens, sniffing, rabbitlike as always. "They say tonight's the biggest thing. If he makes it through tonight, he's going to be okay. He lost an awful lot of blood."

"I know. It's hard to believe."

Dardin shifts uncomfortably on the barstool. "Can we talk about something else, though?"

"Sure, Dardin." Brosius orders another beer.

"Weak stomach, I guess." Dardin rotates his glass upon the bar. "I just can't stand hearing anybody talk about it. That's why I'm so glad nobody could make it out to the site today, and they sent us home. I can't imagine, I mean, seeing it."

Brosius asks, "So tell me about nights then. What's been going on with you?"

Dardin is immediately more animated than Brosius remembers having seen him.

"Well as it happens there's another reason I'm glad to be off tonight."

"Oh yeah?"

"Truth is, I decided to stop in here and settle my nerves a little before I drive on out to see my wife."

"I thought she left for New York."

"Nope. Raytown. Went to stay near her mother after the guy took off and left her."

"You're kidding."

"Nope."

It is the same story Brosius has heard from Dardin before. The woman, night after night in front of the computer screen. The trip to New York State and the announcement of leaving. The children who are not Dardin's, who are from the wife's first marriage to someone before Dardin. The youngest child who is Dardin's. The wife threatening to leave them all.

"She's wanting to saddle me with two kids ain't even mine, and the other one only five years old. Now what kind of woman can do a thing like that?"

Brosius does not know. He shakes his head.

The new ending to the story as Dardin tells it in the bar is that the internet man goes away, changes his email address, and cannot be traced anywhere. Now the kids are with the first father in Topeka and the wife is living with the five year-old in Raytown, a ways south and west.

"So what are you going to do?" Brosius finds, against his will, that he is genuinely interested.

"Well, she called me up yesterday just before I went to work and said maybe we can talk it out."

"And you said?"

Dardin smiles. An even row of small, rounded teeth. He pats Brosius on the shoulder. "That's what I always like about you, Mikey. I tell some of them guys out at the yard she called me, and they can't say nothing but leave that fat so-and-so, and all that kind of stuff. You know how it is."

Brosius can see a flush of color actually moving up Dardin's face, reddening his ears. He remembers only Dardin's quivering black mustache, and that, moving miserably through boxes of parts, he wept easily. Brosius has never seen Dardin blush.

"You love her, though." The words come to Brosius, startling as an accident.

"I do. That's the thing. I love her."

"I know how that is, man." Brosius feels a stinging sense of pain and shock shoot through him, a hot, jittering wire in his back. He imagines the kid, Jimmy Finney. When he watched the ambulance crew moving through the red-slick machinery this morning, lifting the body and laying beside it on the stretcher the twisted and mangled tube of sheet that could only, that must have been the arm, Brosius had been sure the kid was dead. But now Dardin says this is not so, that the kid can still make it through the night. He shudders. Brosius imagines the kid as he will be upon waking, how there will be a white room, perhaps curtains of a window open to the first light of a morning, the moment of happiness swelling in the kid's first breath, then the confusion of place and the moment of hope that will come just before the kid reaches across to touch the arm.

Dardin is staring at him.

"My wife's got a kind of depression mental thing. Genetic. She's not even the same person half the time. She takes her medicine, she's okay, but she says it makes her feel like there's a hole in her head or something. Like she's not there. But every time the quacks go and give her new medicine, they find out some new reason why she can't take it."

Dardin is shaking his head. He had no idea. He does not know what to say.

"The thing is, I stay with her. She hates me half the time, but I stay with her. She says I cheat on her. No matter where I go, what I do, she goes half crazy. I can't argue with her or convince her, but it makes her suicidal if I let her think she's right. I don't know if it makes any difference at this point, sticking around."

Dardin's eyes narrow and he peers at Brosius intently. "That ain't something you can go wrong doing anytime," he says. "Sticking by somebody."

Hours and a few stops later, Brosius is driving Dardin to Raytown in Dardin's car. Dardin chatters incessantly in the passenger seat of the Pontiac. The car shimmies at this speed, the wheel vibrating under Brosius's hands. He focuses on the ribbon of road ahead, but even his vision seems to shake with the engine and the beers from the bar.

By the time they are passing the stadium exit and heading south, it is full dark. Across the highway, Brosius can see the wheel of light that is the stadium. It is the time of year when this could be baseball or football, an ambiguity that appeals to him in this moment of crossing the city. The light of the stadium in the distance, a white wheel along the current of the highway lights.

"Royals are sixty-eight and ninety, can you believe it? Chiefs're doin' good, though. They play the Steelers tomorrow," Dardin says. He speaks into his fist as though it is a microphone, parroting the voice of a famous Pittsburgh

Steelers television announcer. "Here at the convergence of the great waters, these two teams meet tonight."

"Confluence," Brosius says.

"Huh?"

"The place where two rivers meet and run together is the confluence."

"You go to the college of useless knowledge?" Dardin shifts in his seat, animated. Since phoning his wife from the bar to tell her he is off work and can come by early, he has been beaming. Yes, literally beaming, Brosius thinks.

"Hey, why'd you ever leave Arizona to come here, anyway?" Dardin pulls a piece of gum from the pocket of his shirt.

Brosius shrugs inside his coat. "Family, I guess." He rubs first one hand against his leg, then the other. "Your steering is the pits."

"God. I know. I gotta get me a new ride. Me and Shelly get back together, that's the first thing I'm gonna do. Things are gonna be different from now on, I'm telling you. There's gonna be a lot more doing things for me."

Brosius watches the glowing spear of the stadium lights and the white veins of the highway lights recede into the distance, fading to an aura he sees on the horizon in his rearview mirror. Ahead, he exits the freeway and follows Dardin's prompts until they are driving a two-lane highway. The car burrows through a windshield of darkness.

"How far does she live?"

"Not much fu'ther," Dardin promises. "I really want to thank you for coming out here with me, man. I'm so gigged up, I don't think I'd of been able to drive through KC without getting a ticket for sure. I get one more, and like I said before, I lose my license for three months. Then how'm I gonna be able to work and get Shelly to come back home?"

It is okay, Brosius tells him. He understands.

Brosius imagines his own wife, upending a drawer full of his clothing from the balcony of their apartment onto the sparse square of lawn below. The glowing plastic clock Dardin has attached to the dashboard next to the radio informs Brosius that it is 8:43, CST. He rubs his hands along the wheel and keeps driving. There is nothing else to do now.

The house they reach at last is a two-story white Victorian, split into apartments top and bottom. A single, bleary yellow bulb illuminates a sagging front porch, where a badly torn sofa abuts the house. The front door is open, and Brosius can see a hallway full of plastic bags. He parks and shuts off the lights while Dardin twists the rearview mirror to look at himself. He rubs his finger across his mustache and smooths his hair.

"I'd better go up first, just to see how things are going to go. Then I'll come out and get you, okay?"

Brosius nods and stares straight forward at the house. It is somehow too much for him, now, having come all this way—only to find the house, the disrepair, the situation—all exactly as he expected. What may have been at stake for him in finding any of it different, Brosius cannot say. Sitting in the car, he feels something shift as though an invisible tally inside him has checked another item in the damage and loss column.

As Dardin approaches the porch steps, another light comes on in the hallway, defining the silhouette of a woman descending a flight of stairs. The figure, bulky and slow-moving, stands solidly in the door frame, blocking Dardin's entrance. After a few seconds, it moves aside, allowing Dardin to pass. The door shuts, but not before Brosius can see the woman's pale, thick arms, in the porch light, a blowsy nest of hair. Enough evidence to confirm that she is not, cannot be beautiful. He sighs and settles himself back in the seat to wait.

Seconds later, another light comes on, this time in an upper window. Craning to look upward with his head on the dash, Brosius can see a slit in the drapes open to reveal the figure of a small boy, cupping his hands to the window to see out through his own reflection. The boy wears pajamas which Brosius can see, even from here, are patterned with something. Airplanes or cars, probably. The boy looks out at the car in which Brosius sits, and Brosius looks up from inside it, invisible in the darkness. Surely by now the child can hear, inside, the voices of the mother and father. Perhaps he looks to the car below, Brosius thinks, for clues to the degree of permanence in his father's return. Brosius waves. The child does not register having seen him.

In this instant the front door opens again and Dardin comes down the steps quickly, taking them two at a time. He does not get into the passenger seat, but walks around to the driver's side. He motions for Brosius to roll the window down.

"She says she needs me to go with her out to her storage unit tomorrow, and she'll drive me back in time for work. She wants me to stay over tonight and talk things over."

Brosius hears the fatigue in his voice as he answers. "That's great, man."

"You can drive back in my car and just leave it at the bar, or you can sleep a few hours over here if you want. You can sleep in my kid's room."

"That's okay. I gotta get back for work tomorrow anyway."

"That's right." Dardin grimaces. "I forgot about all that. Don't worry, though. Everything's gonna come out just fine in the end, and everything will get back to normal."

Brosius can imagine Crick, pacing in his living room, fists clenched, waiting. Can imagine, in the bedroom, his wife, angelic and sleeping blissfully under an ounce of sedation.

"But if you're tired, you know, you can stay here awhile and just rest your eyes. If them beers is gettin' to ya and you don't think you can make it, I mean. Bad day today."

Dardin is bent over at the waist looking in through the window hopefully, and Brosius motions him away.

"It's okay."

"I'm sorry it ended up this way. I didn't know she'd take me back so easy, you know? But I'm really grateful to you comin' along and drivin' and everything. Like I said, I wouldn't of made it through the city without a ticket, being all wire like I been, and plus a few beers and all."

"It's okay. I'm glad to help out."

"You know how to get back?" Dardin gestures vaguely over his shoulder toward the street. "Right and then left by the Howard Johnson's and then you're back on the highway, right?"

"I'll be fine. I'll leave the car at the bar."

"Yeah. Leave the car at the bar. Good luck, man."

As Brosius backs out of the driveway, he sees Dardin wave briefly before disappearing again into the house. Above, the two halves of the draperies in the upper window cleave inward again and the boy is gone. Brosius turns right, into the night, alone on the road.

As he approaches the city again, Brosius sees ahead of him the fierce eye of the stadium lights spearing upward into the sky. Then, miraculously, as he nears the freeway again, the lights simply shut off, the beam of light erased. He crosses bridges, following backward along the course of the Missouri River before the freeway veers off and he is in the state of Kansas, the city still the same. Somewhere in the darkness, Brosius imagines, the river is growing further away as he drives, its current borne back to a source he does not know.

He is growing sleepy, and as he drives, Brosius plays a game with himself. He could be anyone, Brosius tells himself. Anyone. Nearing his exit, Brosius imagines his children. A boy and a girl, who are at home, asleep, he decides. He has been away on a long trip. He is driving home to them. When he arrives, his wife will be on the couch, where she has fallen asleep waiting. When he wakes her, they will walk softly together, up the stairs of their house to the rooms where their children lie sleeping. He will stand there, with his wife, watching silently the one child turning over onto her side, her lips pursed, gripped by a dream and beginning softly to fuss. In the other room, the other child sleeping heavily, his blanket thrown to one side.

His wife, his children, waiting.

In the very park where he met her, Brosius often stood with his wife, staring upward at the gray-dark sky over the city, seeking stars. They walked the deserted sidewalks and alleyways thick with bougainvillea, oleander and acacia scenting their talk of what it would all be like. Brosius would work for Salt River Project, maybe, after college. They would move to Flagstaff near his parents, or south to Tucson maybe, after that. Somewhere better for raising kids, he had said as they walked past the low, dark shape of a school. Somewhere out of the city where it would actually get dark at night, his wife had said, drifting in lazy arcs on a schoolyard swing and looking up into the city sky. When Brosius thinks of them now, these dreams are as fixed and ever-blooming as everything else ever brought to the desert.

It is too late to make it up with her now, Brosius knows. The fuel gauge on Dardin's car has sunk nearly below E, and he stops two blocks from the bar for gas. Puts four dollars' worth in Dardin's tank and stands staring into the cold case next to the cashier at the convenience store.

"Can I help you, honey?" A woman in a red smock sorts lottery scratch cards behind the counter.

Brosius pulls a box of ice cream sandwiches from the case and sets them in front of her.

She pulls bills from Brosius and counts out coins. "You want a bag?"

"No. Thanks." He pauses. Fiddles with a stack of gum on the counter and looks up into the woman's heavy, mottled face. "You don't happen to know who won the fight tonight, do you?"

Behind her, a television bolted to the wall hangs down at an angle, silently flashing images of car crashes, a bridge collapse, and several close-up shots of frightened citizens which Brosius knows must constitute the eleven o'clock news. The woman looks over her shoulder at the screen and back at Brosius.

"That kid," she says.

"Really?"

"Yep. TKO on the macho in five rounds." She stands beaming at Brosius the way everyone, even leering Menendez, seems to look when they talk about this fighter.

"The great white hope, huh?"

"Huh?" The woman's eyebrows pull upward in a thick arch.

"Nothing. It's great. It's a miracle."

"Miracle shit. Odds were eight to one in favor. Only surprise is him knocking the other guy out. Nobody seen to make odds on that."

That Crick will be there is more than a possibility. The image of Crick's heavy hands and massive arms comes to mind, but the voice, for once, is silent. Brosius feels the cool weight of the ice cream against his hip as he walks back to Dardin's car. Later, in his own car, driving from the bar to his house, Brosius looks at the box, beginning to frost and sweat next to him on the seat. He has heard of how, in hospitals, people can be kept alive on transfusions. The way, if the EMTs get to them in time, people can be emptied out of blood and pumped full of new blood several times, even. It only takes enough blood. He switches off the heater and continues to drive. The kid may be alive. How long could it have taken the ambulance to arrive? Brosius cannot know. It is impossible to read the signs, the complexities of damage. Brosius cannot imagine anymore what will sustain, what may heal. The steering of his own car feels steady and quiet on the road. The ice cream sandwiches, solidly on the seat beside him. He smiles. Ahead, his wife will be waiting. It is for him to bring her the food she likes, the food she is used to.

Animal Control

For days, the emu has circled her house, dropping large flat pies of excrement and divotting the lawn in search of seed. The ghost of Louis Lee himself, a sign her husband is re-created in the afterlife as something ill-formed and roaming the farm. She poses these theories to Donnie Meeks: That if godliness is close to nothing more interesting than cleanliness, what is all the fuss about? That maybe we've all been wrong.

"It won't be the first time," he says. "The bigger question is what takes his place?"

It is unclear whether he means God or Louis Lee. Donnie Meeks worked the small engines line with Louis Lee at the plant. Tall, thin, and twenty-five years old, now he comes weekends to clean up Louis's garage, the spot exactly that the Chevelle, this year's hope for the Demolition Derby Best Painted Car, fell on Louis Lee from its blocks.

Donnie makes repairs and oils Louis Lee's tools.
"You got a rodent problem," he says. He brings live traps for the garage. For her he brings videos on self-defense. He stands in the doorframe, twirling his hat. "A woman alone," he says. "You need to take care of yourself."

In the garage, she picks up the long, aluminum sleeve traps and tips the contents into the 60 gallon aquarium that is quickly filling with mice. She springs the trap doors and sets them again along the perimeter of Louis Lee's garage, empty now without the Chevelle. Into the aquarium she knocks pellets of food and replaces the water drip bottle. Perhaps she can get them a wheel for exercise.

The next morning she picks her way toward the emu, holding out to it in the pre-dawn darkness an offering, small supplication. The bird stares at her through a saurian eye. Its head swivels on a neck long as her legs. What does it want? Why would her response to errant livestock be to ply it with a tray of toasted pecans? She calls Donnie.

Donnie arrives after the emu has nested for the night at the southeast corner of the lot where the hedgerow gives way to winter wheat. Coyotes chitter in the distance. She has been on the phone all day. None of the neighbors are missing a bird. The zoo doesn't want the emu. The sheriff wants to shoot it.

Donnie takes this in with a sigh. "Carmaine," he pushes back the plate from which he has just demolished a slice of her custard pie. "You can't keep living out here by yourself." He will get Animal Control out tomorrow, he says. "And the mice," Donnie reaches for her hand across the table. She winces at the warmth of touch. "It's time to do something about the mice, too."

The emu is making careful progress through the last green shoots around the sewage lagoon when the Creationists arrive with guns.

Reverend Orville Shankland stands on her driveway with his son Toby, directing the boy to aim low as compensation for the rifle's recoil.

"Animal Control is coming," she says.

Reverend Orv looks from her slippers to the housecoat she has wrapped around herself.

"I will welcome you back among us at Kingdom of God, Sister Lee," he says. "I surely will. Meantime, me and my boy's here to help you with your problem."

The boy, fubsy with overweight and layers of woolens takes aim and fires. In the field the emu appears to lift for one second, then come down hopping. It falls and lies flapping. The weight of its useless wings against the air is audible even in the after-ring of the shot.

"Too low!" Reverend Orv sights the boy by the shoulders toward the target. "You shot its damn leg off. Keep your aim where you want to go, in the mass."

She is shaking.

"You go on inside now, Sister Lee," Reverend Orv says. "This whole situation has gone far enough. You need to find your way back into the light."

This time the emu goes down in a heap without a sound. The boy smiles and spits.

Donnie finds her in the garage, a pair of Louis Lee's coveralls zipped over her pajamas.

"I heard what happened," he says.

She feels the warmth of him behind her but does not turn around. "Nothing we can do now."

He uncaps a jar of food pellets and shakes it over the aquarium. "Too many of em. You can't keep them in here like this. Mice carry disease. You know that."

She is crying before she knows it, and when he kisses her it is for an instant like the boy's first shot, earlier that morning. A cold, sick feeling in her stomach. Then, something new, magnetic, animal. She is a forty-three-year-old woman in grease-stained coveralls, standing in a garage. Donnie could be her son, almost, if she had really been pregnant when she married Louis Lee. If Louis was not, as they found out later, unable.

"I can't do it," she says.

"You can do anything," he tells her.

The scrabbling of a mouse along the garage shelves knocks a socket wrench to the floor where it lands with single, ringing metallic note. Go on, Louis Lee, she thinks. Get on where you're going.

They sit side-by side on the tailgate of Donnie's truck, staring toward the bright-lit Kingdom Church and rubbing their hands as if before fire. Silently, he passes the bottle to her. She sips. Heat works through her chest.

"The best part of church," he says. "Being outside it."

Behind the blazing windows, the voices rise in song, swell, and end in the amen.

"You ready?"

"Okay."

"Okay?"

"Yes. I'm ready." She tugs her scarf tighter to her throat and eases off the tailgate. They lift the aquarium, straining together for one moment, then tip it onto the grass of the churchyard. The mice swarm over their feet and are gone. She imagines their path through the grass, over the paving, to the warmth and the light and the sounds of Reverend Orv's voice in the darkness calling, "Here at last, my children, the doors are open unto thee."

Forty-Six Pounds, A Love Story

McManus bought the two-story because it faced south over the canyon. After he knocked out over half of the upper story floor, what remained upstairs, perched on the edge of a loft-balcony, were his office and the bathroom, neither of which any longer had outer walls on the south side. He then knocked out the south-facing wall of the house and replaced it with sheets of glass and glass brick, and the result was that no matter where one stood in the house, one was exposed to an open area downstairs which he had cleared for his photographic studio.

He installed a steep ladder rather than stairs to the bathroom and the office above. Now, in order to use the toilet, he is forced to climb the ladder. And, should the phone ring while he is thus indisposed, he must scramble into his pants and down the ladder again to answer it. This does not make any sense. McManus does not know why he has reconfigured the place in this way, only that it feels right, as though some inner voice is driving him, as though it is trying to show him something.

McManus does not like to miss calls to his land-line from the TV studio where he works as a cameraman for a situation comedy that films weekly. After many near-falls on the ladder, he has installed, next to his office desk, a fireman's pole. With the addition of the pole, McManus feels that the house is shaping up considerably. Downstairs he has maintained the vast, open, well-lighted space he believes is needed for his work. In one corner, each piece laid out meticulously next to each other piece on two folding tables, are the lenses and other equipment necessary for what he refers to as his artistic life. In another corner is the kitchen. Here, in addition to sink, stove, cabinets, and a table, he has rigged the old clawfooted tub that he replaced upstairs with a shower stall. Back under the loft, rather like an enormous train berth, is the space McManus has reserved for his bedroom. The entire area is filled with the largest bed he was able to buy at Mattress Plus.

The new naked exposure, the inability to escape the south wall of windows, does not bother McManus, nor does the fact that while seated, thronelike on the toilet, he is visible to anyone across the canyon who cares to watch him, as well as to anyone downstairs in the house. He lives alone, and, aside from models he brings to the house from time to time, has no visitors whom he might offend. None except his girlfriend.

She comes to visit him once a month in Los Angeles. On these days, he pins sheets from the ceiling of the upper story so as to create a wall that blocks the bathroom from the south windows and the rest of the apartment. Today is such a day. It is two weeks before Thanksgiving, and though he has petitioned her repeatedly to visit over the holiday weekend, or to have him come to her in Kansas City during that time, she has refused.

"An eating holiday is too busy a time of year for me," she says. She is finishing yet another series on barbecue. She tells him he'll have to take her when he can get her.

McManus finishes pinning the sheets to the wire strung two inches from the ceiling across the bathroom portion of the upper story loft. Up here the ceiling slants with the roof of the house, and he has to bend his knees to pinch the corners of the sheets onto the line with clothespins without knocking his head against the roof. He is a large bull of a man, thick through the middle of his body, with slabs of heavy flesh along his back like a Holstein. He twists his curly black hair purposefully over the medallion-sized bald spot at the back of his head, as though to protect it. He is standing naked in the bathroom, having just encapsulated it in a wall of linen, and he looks at himself in the mirror. He picks at his teeth, snarls, then pokes his gums. Above one of his canine teeth, he begins to bleed.

"Shit," he says to no one. "I gotta start flossing."

His girlfriend has insisted he floss more. His teeth are yellowed already from years of smoking, and, she says, smoking or not, he is lucky to even have teeth at his age. He has not smoked for ten years, but he has not flossed, either. He is going to have to start. McManus stands back from the mirror and runs his hands over his chest, feeling the thick hair that covers him like a pelt, then holds the round frontispiece of his belly in his hands. He feels like a pregnant woman. He needs to lose weight. Standing on the scale next to the toilet, still holding his belly as though it will weigh less that way, McManus looks down at the digital number between his feet. Two twenty-one. He squeezes the flesh of his paunch in his hands. He needs to lose forty-six pounds.

McManus swishes mouthwash back and forth in his cheeks and looks at himself in the mirror. When he spits it out, the wash is all froth and a few flecks of blood from where he poked himself. He picks up a box of dental floss his girlfriend left on the shelf next to the sink, pulls a long thread from it, and begins working it between his teeth, causing blood to well up between them. He flosses and spits and rinses and spits. The sink is filled with bloody soap.

"Disgusting," he says to his reflection.

Standing naked in his bathroom behind the sheets, nothing in particular strikes him. McManus does not know that forty-six pounds is the approximate weight of the emergency-exit door next to which his girlfriend sits on the 737 which is preparing for take-off on a runway that is aimed, spearlike, toward him in California. A flight attendant's crackling voice breaks through the substrata of air-compressed noise on the plane to tell McManus's girlfriend that, in the event of an emergency, passengers seated next to emergency exits will be required to remove the doors. If passengers are unwilling to perform this duty, they should ring their call buttons to be reassigned to other seats. Across the aisle from her in the other emergency exit seat is an elderly woman who does not look capable of lifting even six pounds. She does not ring her call button, and neither does McManus's girlfriend. The plane takes off.

Rinsing the sink until it changes from pinkish back to white, McManus remembers the night his girlfriend carved the jack-o-lanterns three years ago. On the second pumpkin she was making a mouth with fangs and the knife slipped, slicing into the meat of her thumb. He remembers how her breath sikked in, in one quick gasp, and the way she squeezed the sides of the cut together, blood dripping through her hands and onto the floor. McManus remembers the taste of the blood as he brought her small white hand to his mouth, and the pulse of her thumb on his tongue. He remembers that moment when he decided, instinctively and without thinking, to love her.

That night, before they carved the pumpkins, he brought her a banana bread. It is one of the things he cooks well. "I was just hanging around, so I thought I'd come see what you were doing," he told her when she opened the door and said what a surprise it was to see him. He worked in Kansas City then, for public television. Nobody he knew made any money. They were all going to be something interesting. Writers, poets, artists. He had a show in a small gallery, and that was where he had met his girlfriend before he brought her banana bread. Before she was his girlfriend. In this before-time she was a red-haired woman who had shown up at the gallery with one of McManus's friends, and McManus had ended up talking to her.

"What do you think of this guy?" he asked, gesturing to the photographs along the walls.

"McManus?" She raised one eyebrow above a blue eye. She swished wine around in her plastic cup and wrinkled her nose. "He's okay. I mean, he's no Mapplethorpe. He has an eye for light, and for beautiful things, but he doesn't disturb."

"And art should disturb?" McManus shoved his hands into his pockets and rocked back and forth from heel to toe, suddenly irritable, needing to move.

"Well it should do something more than lull. I grant you, a lot of what disturbs us is just plain shock value stuff. But I think we're so overstimulated we probably need something slightly askew to make us even see anything at all." She seemed to press her lips to the plastic glass without drinking, and resumed swishing the wine around.

"Don't get me wrong," she apologized. "I've never come anywhere close myself to finding a way of conveying what I think is important in any medium."

"Are you a photographer?"

"No," she said. "I'm a food writer."

"I'm born in the year of the sheep," she told him later at the Chinese restaurant to which he took her after the show at the gallery. "That means I tend to start my relationships off on a sour note."

McManus looked at his place mat, where signs of the Chinese zodiac were pictured with calendar years. "I'm a rabbit," he said.

"Look here." She pointed at the place mat. Under the rabbit it read, Look to the Sheep for your Happiness.

McManus smiled. She smiled. Months later he brought her banana bread.

"Ah, quickbread! This is a gutsy thing to bring a food writer." She pulled back the aluminum foil and breathed along the loaf like a she-animal sniffing a cub. "It smells wonderful."

He had watched her smell foods and products in restaurants and stores and the apartments of friends. Her tongue moistened her lips and she seemed to pull in air from below her ribs before breathing it out slowly and identifying ingredients: clove, turmeric, carageenan, lanolin. The banana bread, he knew, wafted all butter, no shortening. He hoped she would be picking up the fact that he had toasted the walnuts. As she broke a hunk from the end and brought it to her mouth he told her he hadn't had much luck with it, actually. He'd made banana bread for enough women by now that if she rejected it, he was going to stop baking it altogether. "Sort of the coup d'grace if, on my last attempt, I can get it by a fine-tuned palate like yours," he said.

She offered him a bite, which he took, and they both smiled at the warmth and sweetness, the butter and sugar dissolving, the soft crumb of the cake. "You make it sound like a Chrysler," she said. "A person's sense of taste is fine or it's not. There's no tuning involved." He noticed again as he had often felt since the gallery, that sense that she just barely held back a desire to laugh. Her eyes held a kind of light he had observed sometimes when shooting portraits. It suggested a secret, a joke he wasn't in on, but which she might like him enough to let him in on eventually.

Whether she really likes his banana bread or just wanted to tell him so that night, McManus has never asked her. That night, at least, they ate it. She lived in one of the new apartments in reclaimed buildings by the river and the new city market. The area still ticked with tension at night. They heard sirens, the bass-beat of stereos in passing cars. In her kitchen, everything tile and white enamel and wood, they drank coffee and ate and talked.

"I have some pumpkins," she said. "They gave us pumpkins and squashes and gourds out the wazoo at the Pilgrim Fest this year." She grimaced. "All that pumpkin pie. Ech. So should we carve them?"

They carved them. She cut herself. He pulled her to him, before he knew what he was thinking, and kissed her bleeding thumb, took it into his mouth, closed his eyes, and tasted her skin, the coppery red blood, her. As McManus stands at the sink in his loft, the water finally washing clear in the basin, he thinks of that night. He thinks of his girlfriend whom he will pick up at the airport in an hour. The phrase comes to him: Blood of my blood, flesh of my flesh. He is going to ask her this time. He will ask her to stay for good.

McManus cannot know the nexus upon nexus of connections that are woven between him and his girlfriend, those forty-six pounds, that blood in the basin. Ten-thousand feet over Colorado heading west, she is thinking of blood and flesh and bone. She believes in the body more than she believes in anything, though she believes in numerology, astrology, tarot, and runes. Beside her, the number forty-six on the emergency exit door. Four plus six equals ten, which, she thinks, is a good, round number. A seven-thirty-seven is seven plus three plus seven, which is seventeen, an age she remembers as being good. It was the last year she was able to fly in a plane without thinking about it plummeting to earth.

McManus's girlfriend has always believed she is special. Her runes tell her that her essential essence is chaos, the most dynamic of the elemental forces. Her astrological sign is Libra, the eternal feminine of Venus, a symbol of scales balancing head and heart. She tells herself that her connection to McManus is part of the whole astrological, numerological, runic "other plan."

They must belong together. Every way she adds up their ages, their weights, the number of teeth in which they both have fillings, she gets an even ten-derivative or a seven. This is lucky, no doubt about it. Predestination is clear. They belong together. They belong separate. She turns the pronouns over in her mouth like round stones: I am, You are, We are. They are a conjugation.

McManus himself makes no sense to her, not any way she turns him. Not the way he has been or will be. Not the things he photographs, the things he has done to his house. And what is it in the things he has done to the two-story, anyway? She shakes her head, shakes the idea of him almost off.

There are times, though, when she holds McManus's big head in her hands, feels warm blood beating in the temples and looks into those brown eyes, she feels her own self melting into the we like a conversion. As the flight attendants wrest their cart of drinks down the aisle of the plane, McManus's girlfriend is thinking of the truth of the body, that there, in the connection of skin and breath, there is everything. When the cart reaches her she asks for juice. Then, feeling the heat beating in her chest, changes her mind and asks for Scotch.

McManus's girlfriend has always believed she is special, but beyond this, she is. She is one of the few people in the world who can claim to have survived a plane crash. At the age of seventeen, flying to Virginia to visit her uncle Frank who worked for the U.S. mint, McManus's future girlfriend found herself afloat in the freezing Potomac River after the DC-10 on which she had been traveling hit the Wilson Memorial Bridge and spilt its passengers and luggage like seeds from the jagged split of its side, an open pod. She remembers belly-flopping drops as the plane lost altitude, people scurrying, frantic voices on the intercom, a woman forcing her head down between her legs as the engines began to screech with the pilot's efforts to slow the plane. She remembers seeing the banks of the Potomac through the emergency door where she was sitting above the wing. Alongside them, coming impossibly fast, was the western edge of the Wilson Bridge. Cars were driving on it. Then she was somehow in the frozen river, clutching a blue carry-on bag she had never seen before, floating on it, her legs numb, and boats were coming.

By now McManus is at the airport, waiting. He knows she likes for him to be at the bottom of the escalators from the gate. Every time she comes to him it is a small miracle, the way, out of the tunnel of steps, she appears, her hair bright, her eyes squinting and scanning the crowd for him. When McManus thinks of the plane that crashed on the Potomac he feels his stomach turn over, the language of the body that, he believes, tells him he cannot live without her. It had taken a year of dinners and dates before she allowed him to watch her prepare to fly for a weekend junket in Baltimore to judge a crab cake competition. She explained the way she turned over tarot cards. The reasons she picked and turned over marked stones on her bedspread and considered these before packing. She told him about the DC-10. He wanted to tell her he would keep her safe, grounded, but instead he told her he would not leave her. He would water her plants. He would be right here. That first weekend he knocked around her apartment in Kansas City, picking up and setting down objects, marveling at the weight of a tube of toothpaste, the shimmer of bathroom lights on the shower curtain, the heartbreaking vee of a flock of geese he watched through her livingroom window winging south over the river. He thought of her near death, then remembered her life, the warmth of her pale skin, that blood pulsing in her thumb, and around him each thing was brighter, more enigmatic, more vivid with the thought of her having escaped death.

Why he moved away from her to L.A., he tells himself, has nothing to do with her, with that plane. It is his work, his art, the way things happened to go. But when he thinks that she still flies, at least once a month now, to see him, he is amazed. When he sees her, standing in the terminal shifting her shoulder bag and adjusting her glasses, it is as if he will weep at the small miracle of her, just standing there, small in an airport, delivered safe once again.

This time, when she appears in the doorway from the plane, McManus is hiding behind a fat woman wearing a light purple track suit. When his girlfriend turns the other direction, searching for him in the crowd amassed near the luggage carousels, McManus sneaks from behind the fat lady and grabs his girlfriend around the back.

"Ha," he says.

"Ha yourself," she says, startled but smiling.

All the way to the car they twine around each other. On the drive home they touch one another across the emergency brake. Back at the loft house, McManus pulls her toward the bedroom, which is just that: a room that is a bed, and the next time either of them gets up it is to climb the ladder to the bathroom.

"You still like seeing me?" She calls down from upstairs as she flushes the toilet. "Every time?"

He does not answer until he sees her legs coming down the ladder once again—white legs, then the rest of her. The light is blue-dark through the south windows. They have been in bed all day. When she lifts the quilt and slips in beside him, he answers her.

"Of course I do. I wish you were here. Or I was back there. Or somehow, we were together."

When she does not answer, he squeezes her. "Don't you?"

"What I think," she says, "is you should show me how to take a bath in that tub contraption in the kitchen. That's new since the last time I was here."

In the corner of the loft house that serves as a kitchen, McManus shows her how it works. The kitchen faucet gets connected to a hose, which goes into the tub. While it fills with hot water, McManus brings candles from all over the house and lights them, filling the loft with flickering shadows. He pulls a bottle of wine from above the refrigerator, opens it and pours into two jelly jars. Then, before the tub is completely full, he squirts bubbles under the hose. Aside from stemmed glassware, he has forgotten nothing.

Sitting at the kitchen table, his girlfriend grins. She sips her wine.

"Are you coming in?" she asks.

"No, but I'll sit here and talk to you."

When she is in the tub, he tells her, "The good thing about having a tub in your kitchen is you can watch dinner while you soak. Or perhaps you are dinner?" He flings a piece of carrot he is chopping into the bath, and she splashes him.

"If you were here all the time, you could take baths like this and I would cook for you."

"If I was here all the time, I'd end up taking baths by myself and you'd go out to eat."

"Oh come on. That's not fair. You're so pessimistic that people always lose interest, always fall into routines."

"I'm saying I eat for a living. It's relentless. Nobody who doesn't do it can appreciate what that's like. Nobody wants to live with a person like that. We'd probably stop eating together within a month."

"So why doesn't that happen now? Why didn't it happen before?"

She shifts in the water, displacing some onto the floor. "There's a kind of energy, a passion that comes from denial, maybe. We never lived together, and now maybe distance adds a kind of spin on the essential elements. It's like kryptonite or something in the crucible."

The essential elements! Kryptonite! McManus cleaves through a stalk of broccoli. The way she talks can grate on him. It really can.

She is submerged to her chin, bubbles around her face like a wreath. The candles make her eyes glow, and her red hair, twined on top of her head, catches the light like something burning. McManus wants to take her heart-shaped face into his big hands and hold it there, but he continues to chop vegetables he is going to fry in a wok, and she stands up and begins to towel herself as the water drains away through the hose. Watching her emerge from the water makes McManus think of the DC-10 in the Potomac. His thoughts, as always, return to this. This is a woman who fell from the sky, who floated in icy water while a bridge spilled wrecked cars and iron pilings around her. She is barely over five feet tall, weighs little more than a hundred pounds.

If she knew his thoughts now, McManus's girlfriend would tell him she is an "air sign," a sign of light, but she is drying herself, and all he can think of is the long bones of her thighs, the jutting triangles of her hipbones, her white skin in the gold light. She is slim as pared soap, something that could dissolve and disappear in water, but which has not, which has been spared.

"Hey. You can die anywhere, anytime," is what she has told him when he asks her how it is that she can continue to fly on airplanes. "And quite honestly, what are the odds of it happening twice? Like lightning striking. The numbers are against it."

The way she says this, it sounds as if the odds are against dying twice. McManus wonders again whether some part of her feels it has already died, as if she lives now, ghostlike, drifting through her life suspended above her body or beside it, unable to let go. What McManus cannot know is that those moments when she enters a plane again—that place which is neither here, below, nor there, above—those moments of both and neither are the most real moments in his girlfriend's life.

When she finishes toweling off, McManus's girlfriend pulls on one of his shirts. Women know how they look in men's shirts, he thinks. They know how small, how delectable it makes them look. She begins unwinding her hair and pulling it back from her face with two tortoiseshell combs.

"Are you hungry? I could cook now, or we could go outside for awhile." He wills it as strongly as he can, and she answers just as he has wished.

"Let's go outside, she says. She dresses and they go.

Outside, the moon on the east side of the house is rising, low and yellow, a big, fat adenoid of a moon. The patio is paved with jutting, uneven flags that are cracked and filling in with weeds. McManus and his girlfriend sit in webbed chairs, staring up, surrounded by high hedge where some late season insect or night bird is thrumming. The steady burr pulses the night like a heart. The 404 freeway whoosh is a far-off surf.

"It's so yellow. It's beautiful," she says. McManus's girlfriend is waiting for something. She remembers nights they walked lamplit bridges downtown, afternoons they ventured along the river. Los Angeles is so traffic-clogged, so suburban. It is hard to sense the sky here, yet here they are under the moon. She feels the approach of words, low, over the sounds of the night. What she wants is a thing she cannot name to herself, and so she leans her head back to the moonlight as if it will wash over her face like water.

"It's pollution," McManus says.

These are not the words. She sighs. "I know, but it's one of the few perks that comes with smog."

McManus cannot move from the spot where he sits. "So there are things about California you could live with?"

"Some things. Nights like this. Qualities of light in the morning. It's easy to forget about the rest of L.A. up here, above it."

"You could live here." His heart hums in his chest like a tuning fork.

McManus's girlfriend sits back in such a way that the chair creaks and sighs beneath her. "What would I do here? I mean, for a career?"

He leans back upon his hands. "You can write about food anywhere. And honestly, who tries to have a career based in Kansas City these days?" He regrets it immediately, but it is too late.

"Why are you saying this?"

"I don't mean anything. I mean—" He stops himself.

"You think being a food writer is easy? Do you ever have to speak French? Do you have the patience to listen to an obsessed guy wearing a baseball hat with a pig tail and ears tell you the exact technique for smoking a haunch of pork? It's about taking people seriously. Taking their work seriously. And eating it. Spitting all that food into napkins because you can taste it but you just can't, not ever, eat that much. And people will feed you anything. If I never see another chicken it will be too soon. People will do anything to a piece of chicken. Everybody thinks they've got the original fried chicken recipe. Ten years ago people started discovering duck. Now they're trying to do Southern Comfort food. So much of it is so bad. It's unbelievable. I'm off birds completely." This is not how she wanted it to go. McManus's girlfriend stands up and paces the patio flags.

"So why don't you quit? Start over? You could do something else. There are a million things you can do in food, especially out here. I mean, it's competitive, but still. With your experience you could break in. You could do it."

"I like my job. I'm good at it. I like living in Kansas City, and I have a certain sort of small fame in K.C."

This is the line that gets him. He has heard her use it before. A certain sort of small. "You know," he says, "you use an awful lot of alliteration when you talk."

She stops pacing. "So what are you saying? I should quit writing about food because it's making me speak like a bumper sticker?"

"I'm saying," he pauses to make sure exactly what he is saying, "I'm saying you've got a job and a small amount of fame as Gayle Gorton, the food writer. But in reality your name is Julie Minah and you used to say you wanted to be a novelist. I mean, what about the responsibility of art and all that?"

"And?"

"And nothing." This is the point where McManus is supposed to gather her in his arms and passionately proclaim that it doesn't matter what she does, that these issues are missing the point, that he cannot live without her. She is there on the patio, separated from him by only four feet of darkness, and all he can think of is the small shape of her, emergent in the aftermath of disaster. He clears his throat, surprised at the words he hears himself speaking next. "I just think maybe you're not being honest with yourself, doing the food thing. You're selling yourself short."

She walks past him and slams the patio gate. He hears the door to the house slam too. When he follows her, he can see by the billowing sheet that she is standing above him in the loft.

"What are you doing?"

Her face appears behind the sheet for a moment before she pulls it down around her.

"I'm packing my toothbrush," she says.

"God, Julie. Don't do that. All I'm saying is you don't want to sell yourself short is all." McManus walks to the base of the ladder and stares up at her.

From the top of the loft looking down at him, McManus's girlfriend can see nothing so clearly as the small, vulnerable bald spot on the top of McManus's head.

"Not sell myself short? As opposed to you?" The words fall from her like shards. "You left K.C. to live—why—in L.A. You earn a paycheck filming a sitcom and your artistic life takes place under another name completely. I mean, you're embarrassed. You move out here, change your name, and stop producing art completely."

"I am working." McManus's face, looking up below her, goes red as a sausage. "I'm listening right now. I feel a project coming on."

She grips the railing and sniffs. "God, you make it sound like flu or diarrhea."

"Why are you doing this?" His head drops and she looks away out the windows at her own reflection superimposed over the Los Angeles night.

It was true, once, in the beginning. Everybody they knew wanted to be an artist. The questions pregnant in the air for all of them: where they would each need to go, what would be necessary, whether one could come from Kansas and succeed beyond it. But what is he doing? What is she doing?

Her toes are four feet above his head. They stare at each other across the strange new space between them. Below, across the canyon, thousands of lights twinkle like flies, like candles just for them. The silence draws out, deep as a ringing gong.

McManus sees above him the form that is his girlfriend, haloed now in the bathroom light, surrounded by the dropped sheet. She leans over the railing, an angel almost falling. Before he knows what he is doing, as if by instinct, McManus ducks away under the loft floor, the steady flesh of him suddenly gone from her gaze like something borne by a current under a bridge.

It takes two mornings after she leaves before McManus sees it, but the layout of the place is all wrong. The two-story over the canyon, over which he has labored so long, is stultifying. The ladder, the pole, everything, he sees, conspires to spill him downward from above. McManus spends the next two months building the stairs back in and the walls back up. He pulls the bathtub out. When he is finished, McManus sits in the now-smaller downstairs space and looks up at the studs, ribbed across the bottom of the upstairs flooring like the bones of a giant fish. He holds his hands in front of his face, framing this image. It is not bad. Not bad at all.

The only flight out in the early morning when she leaves is from Burbank. But this is not why McManus's girlfriend's return from California is delayed. What happens is that the cooling system of the 737 malfunctions as the plane sits idling, waiting to taxi its way to the runway aiming east. The cabin fills with noxious fumes. When they are finally unloaded, the passengers walk back from the plane across the tarmac. Due to the nature of the plane's malfunction, the travelers are deboarded down stairs, without benefit of an elevated tunnel to issue them from cabin to gate. As she walks to the airport, unsteady under the weight of her bag and dizzy with smoke, McManus's girlfriend turns to look back at the plane. The giant whale shape looms behind her, hulking on the tarmac, spouting funnels of black smoke. She turns again and trudges toward the airport.

The sight of the plane makes her suddenly hungry, though she never eats this early in the day. She thinks of McManus and the crazy split-level house in the canyon, and she shudders. It has nothing to do with art, with anybody's job, what happened back there. She feels herself weightless, drifting. Perhaps it is the smoke she has breathed, or the quiet lightening of the sky as the sun rises. McManus's girlfriend notices that her feet do not touch the tarmac as she walks. She is four feet, now six feet above it and rising. She smiles. It has never been about the food at all, of course, the work of food being, simply, what you take in—a calling of the body, that thing that keeps us here, aground.

Lost and Found

Fat Joyce trailed behind Mr. Christman up the shop steps and into the kitchen where he had fixed to have a smoke. Large hips lolling from side to side, her flanks looked like two slabs of granite liable to grind a small man like Mr. Christman between them. She was panting, and as she gained the top step, Fat Joyce turned and surveyed the parking area behind her as though she had achieved the look-out of some famous monument from which to view the land and people below. She leaned against the door frame so that her terrific weight could be eased from one foot onto the other, and stood with the awful calm of a boulder after a storm. She squinted against the morning sun. The two brown buttons of her eyes, sunk into the great, white cheese of her face took in the bits of broken glass in the lot, the weeds cracking through the sidewalk, and the pile of empty propane cans that lay alongside the shop. She did not hear the finches whistling where they nested in the eaves above her. She snapped her hearing instead upon the sound of Mr. Christman striking a match in the shop.

This room opened through a metal door upon the walk-in refrigerator, and it was this refrigerator, Mr. Christman had informed her this morning, which had been emptied. Seventy pounds of cheese. Forty, seven-pound bags of ground beef. Boxes upon boxes of iceberg lettuce. Boxes of tomatoes. Twenty-three tubs of sour cream. And the salsa. Thirty jugs of salsa in all, twelve spicy, eighteen mild. Whoever had taken it all had expressed no preference for hot over mild. They had come through the window, the shards of glass seemed to proclaim, and now all of it: gone, gone, gone.

Fat Joyce turned and stood blocking the sun in the doorway, her eyes staring dully forward like two pieces of cut glass. She shifted her weight to her other foot in a manner that caused the weak wooden boards of the steps to groan beneath her. Beams of light pierced into the kitchen on one side of her at just the height to flash into Mr. Christman's eyes and leave the negative of her image there. When he closed his eyes, he could see the shape of her head and the bulge of her side drawn by sun upon the blood-flower canvas of his retina. Inside his eye, Fat Joyce mapped the Atlantic Ocean. The light beside her corresponded to the shape of the state of Florida.

Fat Joyce was looking at the remnants of Mr. Christman's tenure as an employee of the Burrito Shop. Outside, across the parking lot by the garage where the Buggy was stored, Fat Joyce's husband Mr. Dimlinger had slithered under the trailer to examine the hitches and safety chains. He was visible only to the waist, the rest of him squashed under the hulking shadow of the Burrito Buggy, but Fat Joyce felt his presence keenly as she turned to face Mr. Christman.

Mr. Christman had lit his cigarette and was smoking it and leaning on the counter with one open-palmed hand. He wore a clean blue shirt and canvas pants, but Fat Joyce perceived a sour smell on him. A man like Mr. Christman was there to do as she told him, like children or dogs. But here he stood, this shop worker, staring at her eye for eye and leaning on the counter in a way that most provoked her. Here was Mr. Christman, sulking in her shop, smoking right in front of her and flicking his ashes onto the floor.

Fat Joyce moved forward just at the instant that something moved in the shadow of the Buggy behind her. Christman could detect Mr. Dimlinger dusting off his pants outside. Mr. Dimlinger was a skinny bald man who wore straw hats all year. He smoked Havatampas, which is what Mr. Christman knew a man did if he wanted to keep a woman from getting near his mouth. Mr. Dimlinger pulled at his pants legs and waved them back and forth at the knees before brushing the length of his legs from hip to shin.

"Chains is all right. Didn't seem to bust the lock, neither," he called to the shape of Fat Joyce's back in the door frame.

She snuffed and shut the door behind her.

Inside, Fat Joyce flipped the electric switch that brought the kitchen overhead on with a flicker and a buzz. She maneuvered herself past Mr. Christman to where the walk-in door stood open and pulled it to. It was a heavy, metal door with a great sliding handle that locked into place from the outside.

"You mean to tell me you saw no one? You slept right through there—" she gestured at the narrow door off the kitchen with her right arm, the flesh swinging "—and you heard no one? No thing you heard?"

Mr. Christman nodded.

Fat Joyce wrapped her arms across herself and pulled at the sleeves of her giant, flowered dress. "You are less good to me than a deaf dog, Mr.

Christman."

Yes ma'am," he said, grinding the cigarette butt under the toe of his boot and then stooping to pick it up and place it in his pocket.

Mr. Christman stared at the walk-in door, allowing his gaze to focus on the latch so that everything, including the great bulk of Fat Joyce, disappeared. Then he opened his gaze slowly, taking in every aspect of the door and Fat Joyce beside it. She had been in the Guinness Book, it was storied in town. Before she had hired the diet coach and gone on all the reduction plans. She had made the town famous. Signs along Route 30 still proclaimed it: Home of the World's Fattest Woman. Now she was merely fat. Mr. Christman felt a twinge of sympathy for Mr. Dimlinger, outside.

Mr. Dimlinger had married a woman large as a frigate, and there was a kind of fame in that, too, for Fat Joyce was that ship set sail, pigeons jamming her escutcheons, on a motorized cart each holiday down the main street of town. Pink ribbons for Easter. Green for St. Patrick's Day. Sewn into a giant red suit for Christmas. Fat Joyce had been the heart, the great, round heart of the town of Peadro. She had blushed through television interviews alongside Mr. Dimlinger. Mr. Dimlinger, wearing his straw hat at a rakish diagonal, had told the world what it took to keep his sweetheart in sweets: four whole pies for breakfast alone. Whole kitchen sinks-full of tapioca pudding. Once, Mr. Dimlinger told the world, he had, in a pinch, doused several loaves of Wonder Bread with maple syrup. You had to improvise, he said. Improvisation was key. Fat Joyce had blushed and blushed.

Mr. Christman felt a kind of swoon come over him now as he thought of it—to be the greatest something, the greatest anything in the world. What would that mean? Mr. Christman turned around and ran tap water onto his wrists. He savored the cold water and the metallic smell from the pump. Then he turned to face her again.

She had lost weight. Not enough to become simply Joyce, but enough to become merely Fat Joyce. Not the fattest woman in the world. And now, a mere two days before the State Fair, it appeared that she was no longer set to rake in the greatest yearly gold mine of vending money in the county, either. Mr. Christman thought of the empty space in the walk-in behind the door, and then looked at Fat Joyce, staring directly at her eyes.

"You are less good to me than a child in a candy shop," she said.

"I suppose that's so," he said.

Mr. Christman was neither a child nor a dog. Fat Joyce fanned one hand at him as if waving away a fly. The Burrito Buggy, with only thirty-eight boxes of tortillas and nothing to fill them, was not a candy shop, either. Fat Joyce sighed heavily. Through the closed door of the shop she could feel the presence of Mr. Dimlinger in the parking lot. Poking under the Buggy, upturning propane tanks, and spearing pieces of paper with a stick. He thought to find a clue, she knew, and the sleuthing of Mr. Dimlinger outside and the sulking of Mr. Christman inside prickled under her great skin like a rash.

"You cannot think where a person would store this food?" she asked Mr. Christman.

"Maybe they dumped it all. Vandals. They could of dumped it at the narrows."

"But that is not what happened." Fat Joyce moved past him and pushed the door open, spearing him in a beam of sunlight like a trout. "Mister Dimlinger!" she called to her husband, who now sat primly on the Burrito Buggy trailer hitch smoking. Smoking was a habit she could not abide. "Mister Dimlinger, we need to get finding the food now. The Fair is in two days."

"Buttercup," he said, "I'm afraid those boys whatever did it is long gone by now. Ain't a clue to they whereabouts."

She made her way down one step, then the next, and across the parking lot toward him. She was slow, but she was steady. He would give her that. Fat Joyce was the rock, not the sand.

Mr. Dimlinger found Mr. Christman that afternoon at the Pink Pig Pub on Highway 30. Mr. Christman ate deviled eggs and sipped from a beer while Mr. Dimlinger talked and gestured with his hands.

"She's going to find it, you mark my words."

Mr. Christman pushed another egg half into his mouth and shrugged his shoulders.

"She will sniff around and poke around until she finds it. Ain't nothing come between that woman and food, she won't find it." The woman never would, he thought, listen to a damn thing he said. She would drive herself all over the county in the rumbling yellow Buick with reinforced floor boards and special, steel-belted radials. She would heave herself up one set of steps and the next, if need be. Slowly and steadily, one way or another, the woman would foil his plans. Fat Joyce was the tortoise, Mr. Dimlinger thought, not the hare. Mr. Christman dabbed his mouth with a napkin and sipped from his beer again. The velvet yolks of the eggs dissolving in his mouth and the cold bitterness of the beer brought a warm gold to his chest.

"Who you're talking to is an unemployed man." He pushed his bar tab toward Mr. Dimlinger and felt the gold spread through his arms and torso like a stain.

Dimlinger snatched the slip of paper. "Fine. That's just fine, then." He pulled two bills from his wallet and laid them on the bar. Then he pulled more bills from his wallet and counted them against his thigh. "One, two, three, four, and five is a hundred. That's a hundred showed up front, a hundred later."

Mr. Christman took the money and folded it into his shirt pocket without speaking.

"Plus three eggs and a beer." Mr. Dimlinger scanned irritably around the Pink Pig. Only one man in the place besides themselves, and he was sleeping in a booth with his back to the door. Verlene, the day bartender, leaned over the juke box, punching numbers. She did not look up.

"What's happened to service in this world?" Mr. Dimlinger rubbed his sleeve across his face and wrinkled his brow at Mr. Christman. "She ain't even turned around since I come in here. A paying customer, no less."

Mr. Christman nodded. He smiled.

Music blared suddenly through the Pink Pig, the plaintive wail of a singer named Johnny Lee Handover, a local boy from Riggs who had hit it big. Only two towns over, Mr. Christman thought. He had seen that Johnny Lee a few times at the State Fair as he had stood warming tortillas on the flat iron of the Buggy oven door. Mr. Christman had listened to Johnny Lee Handover sing this very song. From the trailer hitch, he had been able to see the left part of the stage where every few minutes Johnny Lee paced with his microphone, tipping his black hat and crooning, "broken heart and barbwire… " Johnny Lee Handover in snakeskin boots and leather pants, wailing over a crowd of girls that undulated beneath him like a sea. Mr. Christman had thought then the boy might amount to something. It was a thing, that's what it was, to hear him on the radio now. A boy from Riggs. Mr. Christman sipped at his beer and watched Mr. Dimlinger light another tiny cigar. People did the most amazing things. You just never knew, he thought. You never did. He lit a cigarette of his own and smiled at the sound of the music and the sight of smoke, his own and Mr. Dimlinger's, ribboning over the two men in the gold-yellow light of the bar.

"Salvation," he said to Mr. Dimlinger. "Song's called 'Salvation.'"

Fat Joyce stood with her hands on her hips. But for the great heaving of her chest as she panted, she might have been a stalagmite, splintered up through the floor as she stood amid the shavings of broken wood and glass. Here was the block of cheese it was for Mr. Christman to have garrotted into bricks and shredded. In front of her on the floor sat boxes of head lettuce, tubs of sour cream, and whole tomatoes stacked like hearts into two great pyramids. Behind her, testament to the great, splintering bulk of her will stood the door of Mr. Rafael's vending shop. The lock, sundered as if by a wrathful bolt from on high, lay in a twisted knot where it reflected the overhead light in a dull metallic wink. The up-turned trash barrel lay just behind her feet, spilling wrappers and cellophane. Fat Joyce stared into the fluorescent glow of Mr. Rafael's walk-in refrigerator, sagging with supplies for his buggy, the Hamburguesa. She wiped her palms against her hips.

She thought of Mr. Dimlinger's straw hat. Mr. Dimlinger with a toothpick in his teeth. Mr. Dimlinger smoking on the stoop. Here it was, just as easily as she might have imagined it. Fat Joyce shuddered in the umbilical of light from the refrigerator. Alongside the wall of Mr. Rafael's shop stood box upon box of buns and ketchup dispensers and mustard tubes. On the walk-in shelves stood huge plastic jars full of green relish, boxes of burrito ground beef, burrito salsas hot and mild, and of course, the cheese. Her cheese.

Mr. Dimlinger was a man, that was all. She stood with the blood thrumming through her legs, kneading the soft flesh of her neck in her hand, and somewhere beneath, the butterfly thyroid in her throat. The whole thing weighed upon her immensely, alternating between wrath and mercy. What was to be done? A parakeet she could love. Fat Joyce admired parakeets of all colors-lavender and bunting blue for Easter, sunny-side-up yellows and kiwi greens. She had kept seventeen parakeets in her house. The birds hopped from table to plate as she ate, leaving fork-shaped bird tracks in the potatoes and meat loaf. She had fed them scraps from her fingers, lifted birds to her shoulders and the fierce net of her hair. Fat Joyce loved parakeets. But a man? This was something else. A man was less than a parakeet. Like a slow-moving river fish or turtle that had remained the same, unevolved, for generations. A man was a bottom-dwelling, self-loving thing.

Sugar Pop and Sweet Biscuit, he had called her. He had sat in the swing of the sagging front porch and sipped lemonade and strummed a ukulele like a seersucker crooner in a movie. A man with a tiny guitar, this Fat Joyce did not trust. Mr. Dimlinger with his straw hats and cigarillos and his little guitar that sounded out notes like rocks plunking into a well. You could marry a man, people said. You could not marry a parakeet. Fat Joyce had married Mr. Dimlinger, and Mr. Dimlinger had given all the parakeets to Woolworth's. The thought of those bright birds on the tables and curtain swags, and the thought of Mr. Dimlinger in her kitchen, wearing his apron and holding out to her his gold-plated spoon sent a flutter to her stomach and set up a great growling there.

Fat Joyce turned and moved through the debris in Mr. Rafael's shop, pulling a box of ground beef behind her like a barge through ice. There were two skillets on the wall above Mr. Rafael's range. She eyed them steadily, still holding one flap of the box. Five pounds of food per skillet at least, she estimated. She pulled each one from its hook and set them on the burners, one and two. Fat Joyce tore through the clear tape binding the box, through the plastic bags beneath, and into the soft, cold weight of the meat. It was clear what could be done. It was bright as day. Between her hands she began pounding and shaping the flesh into disks, and laying them one by one into the skillets.

In the Hamburguesa Buggy shop, Mr. Rafael swept short whisks along the floor with his broom. They were gone. The wrappers and cellophane and boxes, the crumbs of yellow cheese, the tomatoes split into empty skins, the greasy iron skillets and sheaves of torn lettuce leaves. Mr. Rafael had swept and scrubbed the debris into bags. He had stacked the bags into the city truck and watched it drive away. Along the wall, untouched, were the packages of buns and the condiments: mustard, ketchup, relish. Rafael swept his way in short strokes to the end of the room, and pushed the line of dirt out the shop door. He paced the length of the shop and began again, sweeping.

Outside, framed in the rectangle of open doorway, Mr. Dimlinger stood talking to Sheriff Lipton in the waning afternoon light. Through the line of trees behind Mr. Rafael's shop, the sun made small gold specks like a thousand birds, moving in the leaves. The sheriff wrote with a pencil onto a pad of paper while Mr. Dimlinger pushed his hat back upon his forehead and looked up toward the sky. Mr. Rafael watched the sheriff snap the pad closed upon itself and place the pencil in his pocket.

"A thing like this, it just boggles the mind," Sheriff Lipton wheezed.

"It does at that," Mr. Dimlinger said.

Sheriff Lipton shook hands with Mr. Dimlinger and called around him to Mr. Rafael in the shop, "It's a tough thing coming right before the Fair and all."

Mr. Rafael merely watched as the sheriff walked away toward the cruiser which sat idling in front of Mr. Rafael's red buggy, El Hamburguesa.

"Some things," Mr. Dimlinger called after Sheriff Lipton, "are just beyond the common man." He watched the car drive away, then climbed the steps and stood watching until Mr. Rafael stopped sweeping and leaned against his broom.

"No criminal charges, under the circumstances." Mr. Dimlinger struck a match against the back of its book. He allowed it to burn down between his finger and thumb before tossing it out the shop door and lighting another in the same way.

"I would not have filed, of course." Mr. Rafael pulled a folded bill of sale from a trouser pocket beneath his apron and handed it to Mr. Dimlinger.

"Under the circumstances."

Mr. Dimlinger's eyes narrowed. He did not move.

Mr. Rafael set the broom aside, walked forward, and placed the receipt in Mr. Dimlinger's hand. "It's not right."

"She's gone to a better place," Mr. Dimlinger said. A tiny smile revealed the sharp yellow points of his teeth in the red creases of his face.

He looked, Mr. Rafael thought, like a rat. If you saw a rat in the day time, his father had once told him, you stayed away from it. It was rabid. Mr. Rafael stood surveying the clean empty lines of the hamburger shop and the red, rat face of Mr. Dimlinger.

"She was right there." He gestured toward the range.

Mr. Dimlinger shook his head. "Don't dwell, son."

"The burners were still on, but the pans she took down with her when she fell. The whole place would have gone up."

"When you can't change a thing, it ain't good to smart over it." Mr. Dimlinger placed the book of matches and the bill of sale into his shirt pocket. "It's over."

Mr. Rafael thought of the great pine box that would be needed. A packing crate of some kind, he imagined. Fat Joyce had been rolled like a sea lion to one side, the blanket shoved under her, then rolled the other way like an awkward piece of furniture. The crew had rolled the great leaking bulk of her flesh onto the cloth and pulled her to the door, then unceremoniously down a ramp of plywood laid over the steps and into the truck.

"She must have hated you," Mr. Rafael said. "Or loved you. It is hard to say."

Mr. Dimlinger squinted as if thinking. "Gives the body a chill, don't it?"

Mr. Rafael walked over to the stove and squatted down onto the floor. "There is a place in Texas I saw once. They have a seventy-two ounce steak there. If you can eat it in an hour, you can have it free. But it is not just the steak. They give you potato and salad and dessert and a drink. You have to finish it all. Not just the steak. Everything. They have people watching the whole time to make sure you don't cheat and put some in your pocket."

"I heard of that before." Mr. Dimlinger leaned against the counter on the opposite wall, sliding down slowly until he sat in a squat across from Mr. Rafael. "How many pounds is that, seventy-two ounce?"

"About four and a half."

"Four and a half." Mr. Dimlinger whistled through his teeth. "How much you think is in a box of beef? Four, five bags?"

"About that. Seven pounds each."

"Thirty-five pounds a box." Mr. Dimlinger whistled again. "It makes a body just shudder, don't it?"

Mr. Rafael stared along the line of the floor to the open doorway where the sun pierced inward in one yellow shaft, glinting against the sprung hinges. He felt a chill when he thought of it, to be endowed with—what? Such an ability? It was massive. What would it be, to have this—this—be one's gift from God? He shook his head. "They ought to have said something before they took her away."

"They did. They said holy shit." Mr. Dimlinger stared in the direction of the swaying trees behind the parking lot. "Don't take it so hard, son. It ain't a thing we could of seen." He raised himself slowly. His knees popped and he exhaled hard. Mr. Dimlinger pulled a wad of bills from his pocket and counted them, smoothing each one onto the counter top. "It's all there but fifty. I imagine you'll be wanting that by and by."

Mr. Rafael waved him away.

"All right then. Be seeing you." Mr. Dimlinger pulled his hat down over his forehead and turned toward the door. More of his joints popped audibly. "See you around, now."

Mr. Rafael watched him go, then stood again and took the broom in hand, sweeping again in small whiffs across the floor. "Amazing Grace," he thought. "How sweet the sound. That saved a wretch like me." As a boy when he had learned the hymn, he had thought of the verse as being about a woman named Grace. There had been one Grace in Peadro then, a large neighbor two doors down, Grace Fitzsimmons, who served lemonade in spotty glasses. Amazing Grace. Mr. Rafael smiled and drifted with the movement of sweeping, forth and back, back and forth. The hymn fit with the rhythm of the broom and Mr. Rafael began to sway slowly in the beams of light that penetrated the empty shop. He faced the metal door of the walk-in refrigerator and touched the fingers of his right hand to his head, his right collarbone, his left.

"Miraculoso," he whispered. "Celestina." There was this day a woman lifted to the bosom of God.

The Wedding Gift

Wish in one hand, my mother used to say. Then spit in the other. See which one fills up faster.

Standing beside her snapping beans to can, or setting the table for supper, I told her about things I had learned in school and things I thought I would like to be besides a farmer and a rancher. Forks on the left, spoons and knives on the right. Cloth napkin quartered into a triangle on each plate. I understood my place in my mother's house, but I had dreams, I told her. The world, I was learning, was large and complex.

I wanted to go to college. I thought I would be a writer, but it's just as well, all things considered. I married a woman who had gone to the local university to be a teacher. Linda. She is part of this story, but before her, what I did out of high school was go to work for Bristol Manufacturing. We made windshield scrapers out of plastic, and waited for layoffs during mild winters. This is Emporia, Kansas, the industrial Midwest, and as jobs go, Bristol was decent. Nothing came in alive and went out in packages. The job did not involve an odor. I worked there eight good years, and I've harbored no bad feelings about it.

What I do now is this: I am a caterer, event planner, and supplier of wedding and event accessories. Or, to put it more precisely, I own the Bow and Box on Commercial Street, across from the diner. I inherited the place from my mother's best friend, Mrs. Parsons, a large woman with goiter and one cloudy eye. Throughout my life, Mrs. P. kept sweets wrapped in napkins in her pockets for me. She arrived in my mother's house smelling always of vanilla.

Mrs. Parsons is buried in Garnett next to Mr. Parsons, who died in an accident some thirty-five years before her. My own mother spoke the final words at Mrs. P's grave site and tossed in the first handful of soil before turning away, dusting her hands on a handkerchief.

"Dirt," she said. "You spend your whole life cleaning it up. You die, and they throw it in your face."

My mother had been close to Mrs. Parsons, who spent every evening in my mother's kitchen for as long as I can remember. Each night I set an egg cup for Mrs. P. She arrived from her job fanning her thick throat and milky eye with both hands, making fatigued exclamations. Like my mother, she did not pray over the plates. She said, Gracious! Do pass the potatoes! Mrs. Parsons listened to my school reports on the space shuttle and the Colobus monkey, my dreams of becoming an astronaut or explorer.

Mrs. P. told me that life was what happened when you were making other plans.

At the funeral that day, I knew I should offer comfort, but Linda had just left me, and I could think of nothing to say. As if in response to my silence, my mother turned and pulled an envelope from her purse and slapped it against my chest.

"Didn't have kids or kin of her own. She liked you. God knows why."

The sheet of paper told me two things in Mrs. Parsons' loopy script. The first sentence said, Your father was somebody your mother met once. The second said, Get on with your life.

Also in the envelope was the title to the Parsons catering business and the lease for the storefront on Commercial Street.

Plenty of people still call us the old Parsons place, though we've overhauled and diversified considerably, and our services are much in demand. Such demand you might think would not extend all the way to my ex-wife and her plans to marry an ostrich-boot wearing real estate agent from Kansas City, but you'd be wrong. Despite my line of work, I myself do not believe in weddings. I was married at the JOP in Hays, to Linda Lewis, light of my life. She did not take my name, but she did take my stereo four months later when she left for Denver with a guy named Tobey who was best known in these parts for his slapstick antics as the driver of the First Aid car in the demolition derby. The car was a souped-up station wagon with a coffin on the roof called "Hillbilly Ambulance."

When she served me papers six months after that, Linda was living in Boulder with a welder she called "Tice." Unlike Tobey and, I could only assume, unlike me as well, Tice, she said, "really knew how to communicate." I met him only once, outside the same courthouse where Linda and I had been married. Before hugging me goodbye for what I assumed would be the last time, Linda stood on the running board of the man's Chevelle, pointed to his bicep resting on the window frame and said, "This is Tice." He gunned his engine several ear-throttling blasts, she hugged me, and then they were gone, just two lines of burned rubber and a whirl of trash and dust funneling their wake. I did not expect her to enter my life again.

I should say right now, including and beyond everything that has happened, I loved Linda Lewis. From the first time I saw her, a sweet co-ed stumbling drunk down Mechanic Street with several of her girlfriends, singing, to the last time I saw her driving away in a $40,000 Ford F-150, married to another man. After all my brooding years alone, she was a bright spot on the dark slope of my conscience. She was ease to Job. She was water after drought. Not that I ever said any of these things to Linda, not even close. But I thought them, and I think them still, how tricky the words are. The need to find the right ones chokes tight as a scarf around your neck all night, and then they come out as inconsequential as smoke when you finally speak them.

I grew up in north Lyon County on the Chase County line. My mother's family farmstead, just me and her and Mrs. Parsons, who had moved into the Smithson family place due south of us. My mother, like me, was an only child. Like her parents, she had been born in the house, and she would die in it. I had no uncles, no aunts, no cousins. No sisters or brothers. No father. Only the promise from my mother that someday, when I was ready, I would know everything I needed to know about him.

Neighboring farmers and the fathers of my friends, various men helped my mother with our land, plowing, pasturing cattle, mending fence. They tried to bring me up right. They taught me how to hold a rifle, how to spit a seed or a wad of phlegm so it would fly out away from an open truck window. They told me things like Measure twice, cut once, and Don't fix it if it aint broke.

My mother met them all in the same way, on the back porch. She stood with her hands on her apron pockets, strings of gray hair blowsy around her eyes, and waited until they removed their hats. She handed over checks or asked to see parts of the tractor that would need replacing. She ran her fingers along the threading of pipe and frayed wiring and said, always, "I'll get back with you." She never invited them into the kitchen.

She had been beautiful once—a round face and light hair piled on her head like a souffle. Pictures in our attic proved this. I had laid these out in rows as a child, unwrapping the glass-fronted faces from layers of drapery in a cedar chest. In the jutting chins of great grandmothers and grandfathers, I looked for my own face. There were pictures of several babies, but each generation had succeeded in bringing forward teenage portraits of only one child.

I watched the men who farmed our land watch my mother coaxing a pullet from the scratch pen or hoeing up weeds. They said things like, Never buy the cow if you can get the milk for free, things I understood had to do with me and the man whose face was not in any of the pictures in the attic.

It was when I met Linda that I saw for the first time the image of the man I might become. A man who would say and do the right thing. I had dated girls over the years, sure. A burger and some beers after work, the moment of standing between your car and hers, each of you with your keys in your hand, waiting for a sign. But nothing like this stupefied love-sickness had happened to me. I wanted to tell Linda herself, tell everyone, that I was feeling things for what seemed like the first time.

I wanted to express myself to her, but she was an educated girl. Each time I tried to say, I love you, or Will you marry me, it came out mangled, twisted. I told her things like, I wouldn't kick you out of bed, or There is always an extra slot in my toothbrush holder.

In these moments, it seemed to me that I could actually see my words just hang there in the air between us. Useless, the neighboring ranchers would have said, as tits on a warthog. Hopeless, my mother would have said, as a hat on a dog.

How I asked Linda, finally, to marry me, was by not speaking at all. I put all of my savings, and they were considerable, living with my mother as I had all those years, into a single diamond solitaire. This I buried in a meatball at S'ghetti's. It's true that she was given the Heimlich maneuver by two of the kitchen help, and there was some cleaning to do of the ring, but in the end she said yes.

She stared up at me from the checkered booth and said, "Oh my god. You're the only guy who ever wanted to marry me so bad you nearly choked me to death."

It wasn't the language I'd hoped for, but it would do. We were married near her parents' place in Hays the next week. She and I and my sound system lived in a trailer on some land of her uncle's for the next four months. I have not seen the ring or the stereo again. Linda herself, however, came into my life walking up the same stretch of Mechanic Street that I had watched her stumble down all those years before.

She had called me and asked me to meet her at the diner on Commercial, which is where I sat watching her approach. She was a little too tan, her jeans too tight. Her voice when she sat across from me in the booth a little too loud. She told me it was good to see me, and she told me how glad she was we had this chance to talk.

"I didn't want you to read about it in the Gazette," she said.

She told me she was living in Kansas City now. She'd met a guy at a Chiefs game. Her eyes glistened and winked as she described how they were both wearing ESU shirts, her alma mater. She told me she'd met fellow Hornets everywhere since leaving Emporia, but this time...

"Whoa, Nellie," she said. This time she was in love.

Linda's Hornet had majored in business. He sold real estate in Olathe. He was teaching her to golf.

I asked her the obvious question. "Why are you here?"

His family was mostly from Reading, all ESU alums. Her family, none of whom I could remember going to school anywhere, was coming in from Hays. The plan was to have a country wedding just outside Emporia. In June. She had not asked me anything since she sat down, so I told her what I thought she would want to know, which was that I was okay with that, and I wished her good luck. I told her I was still living out at mom's house. That I'd got Mrs. Parsons' shop, and it was doing very well.

"That's great," she said. "I'm really happy for you. And I want you to know that if there is ever"—here she paused—"ever anything we can do for you, if you ever wanted to leave this area, try real estate or whatever, Blake I would for sure help you get started."

I felt something else entirely, but I told her that I felt the same way. In fact, I said, I'd love to do something for her. And before I knew it, words just flew from my mouth. I told her to let me take care of the wedding cake and the reception.

"You're in KC," I said. "This way, you would not have to worry about a thing."

"Not a thing?" She twirled a lank of blonde hair around her finger and cocked her head to one side. "Are you serious?" I saw the same half-eager, half-mistrusting expression she had given me during the four months of our marriage just before she asked me if I wouldn't mind buying her something or loaning her my car. It occurred to me, stupidly, suddenly, that she must have had this in mind all along. Still, a thing promised is a thing promised. Of the two of us, I was the one who had kept his word.

"Not a thing," I told her. "I'm serious. Let me take care of it all."

She told me how grateful she was and what a great guy I was, but her final words before leaving the diner in a wake of perfume were a warning.

"Just, please"—she blinked her eyes twice. "Please just—"

"What?"

"It's nothing."

"What?"

"This wedding is really important to us. It's not about you and me. I just don't want this cake thing to become an obstruction."

At this point she waved out the window, and as if he'd been sitting in it all along, a guy stepped down from huge glistening truck with a chrome cow catcher. I saw first a pair of ostrich boots and then the rest of him, all biceps and big thighs. I sat in the window of the diner, watching them climb into their pickup. Despite everything she had been and still was, all I saw was Linda, limbs and blonde walking away from me once again, the curves and clefts of her.

Linda, you are the only one for me, I thought as I took two sugar packets and banged them against my wrist.

My happiness in this life is a bird, beating in the cage of your closed hands, I thought as I tore the packets open and stirred them into the cold coffee.

You are still connected to me, I thought as I nodded imperceptibly, my head dipping the bill of my hat in acknowledgement of their truck as it pulled away.

I imagined them in the air-conditioned cab, the way Linda would be sitting in the center of the leather seats, her hand on his thigh, the way she would be saying right now, "He's so repressed he wouldn't know an emotion if it jumped out of that cake and bit him."

Linda, I thought. What language is it that would tell you all of this? Why don't you see?

I said nothing. I walked across the street to the shop and called my staff together. There are three of them, in addition to the day prep guys and the delivery and serving staff. Three who have been with me from the beginning.

Herb Sugarman has been here since the day after Mrs. Parsons' funeral, when he showed up wearing an orange hunting cap and holding a cross bow in one hand. When I'd told him about my idea for the Bow and Box, he'd been in mind of something else entirely. "This is the Parsons place," he said. "This is the job?"

I'd known Sugarman at Bristol. He mixed the chemicals and set the machines and the flow of plastic that would become windshield scrapers. Sugarman knew by the texture of a production run just exactly what it lacked. He could smell when a batch had too much color additive. He could taste whether coffee in the break room was sweetened with Aspartane or Nutra-Sweet.

Sugarman understands the architecture, the chemistry of catered food. People think it is Mrs. Parsons' recipes, but Herb Sugarman is my secret weapon. You would not think this to see him. He is a big man, barrel-shaped.

He wears Carhhardt coveralls over his kitchen whites and rumbles southward each night in a rusted Dodge flat bed with a cracked windshield. Sugarman's wife was killed I don't know how many years ago on the Americus Road. A white cross at the ess-curve marks it still. Sugarman says he's never seen it, and won't drive the road. He claims his first wife was the last woman for him. Converged upon by well-meaning widows, he sold their house, took the insurance money moved out to Hartford in a trailer with no stove. "A woman won't move where she can't cook you something," he says.

The kid came from Bristol too, right after Sugarman. Pedro. I'd seen him around the factory. He worked in packing and shipping, the first group to get laid off in a warm winter. Pedro takes a lot of classes at the Vo-Tech. He's the one with all the ideas about business and distribution, and he's the only person in the shop who wears a tie.

Starting out, he cleaned the front of the shop and re-fitted gaskets in the kitchen. He answered right up when I asked him, Pedro would you stop down to Muckenthaler's and get some steam trays? Or, Pedro would you mind checking the dates on the flour?

You can imagine our feeling when Sugarman and I looked up from assembling a tray of petit fours one day to see the kid standing there with his hat in his hands, telling us he was sorry but we needed to know his name was Cory, and he needed to fill out some W-4s.

We had called him Pedro for years at Bristol. It had been embroidered on his uniforms.

"When did this start?" Sugarman asked.

"It's always been my name," the kid said. "People around here just take one look and it's Pedro or Paco or Carlos."

I told him he should have said something sooner, and he said jobs for Mexicans were hard enough to come by in a town like Emporia.

I told him it was going to be a challenge after all this time, but we'd learn it.

Regina is Cory-Pedro's sister. She is the one who fills the front windows with bolts of voile, lacy garters, ribbonned boxes spilling perfumed soaps and note cards. Regina is a coffee-skinned woman whose black hair hangs to her waist in waves. At the corner of one large brown eye, she has tattooed a single tear.

Regina sits on a lavender silk cushion by the cash register and nods at the customers. She knows how to talk to women about their weddings—why tiny packets of bird seed are ecologically better than throwing rice. What are reasonable expectations for an ice sculpture.

The tear, it took her a long time to tell us, commemorates her ex-boyfriend Rodney. Rodney had been killed when his car stalled on the railroad tracks in northern Arizona. He was coming back from a construction job in Surprise, she said. What got to Regina wasn't the accident. Rodney was a drunk, she said. It was the way the Phoenix police had broken the news to her by handing over a newspaper clipping from the regional roundup page—a photo of a mangled car under the single word headline, "Surprise." She claims not to have read a newspaper since.

They're good people, these three, and I depend on them to move us from concept to reality. They make the wishes of our customers come true, help them to express their desires in sugar and ribbon and an audio-and-lighting package of thirty-two karaoke devotional hymns.

After my meeting with Linda, I crossed the street and broke the news, my own wish. I had known it since Linda had said her last words to me about the cake, but I had not spoken it aloud, even to myself, until just then.

"We're doing a Princess of Wales," I told them.

Sugarman hooked his thumbs into his apron and frowned. Regina squinted as if against a shaft of sunlight, and Cory adjusted his tie.

We had discussed the cake plenty of times since Bride Quarterly had published it as their cover feature—the architecture involved, the layers of ganache, the enrobing, crystallized violets, candy pearls. The sheer art of a thing done on such a scale.

You could have wiped Sugarman off the ceiling with a mop. "You're joking," he said. "For who?"

"My ex-wife," I said.

Cory told me that I was committing the financial quarter and more resources than we had, and I knew it.

"Surely a Duchess of York," he said. "Or even the Jackie Onassis II would be enough."

Sugarman agreed. "There's a time and place for that cake," he said.

I knew they were right, and yet somewhere between the window of the diner and the front door of the shop, I had decided that time was now.

Over the next few weeks, Sugarman worked from the Bride Quarterly drawings, projecting them full scale. He made models and tasted buttercreams. Regina and Cory did all the correspondence with Linda, the invitations, the color schemes, all of it. I brooded and dropped things and burned myself pulling miniature quiches from the steam-tray. It was a Saturday, morning prep, and I was staring at the schedule without seeing it: the Ladies' salad luncheon, salmon croquettes, the Episcopal assorted pastry tray and punch, weenie-wraps for the VFW and the Cattlemen's brisket barbecue. I stopped with a pair of tongs raised in my hand.

"I need a drink," I said. "On the clock."

We left the staff to finish a tray of petit fours and truffles and headed straight for the smoke and paneling of the Town Royal and the underwater, mid-range frequency of several pitchers of beer drowned in a few choruses of bourbon.

It was getting to me and they knew it. I told Sugarman and Cory everything I hadn't told Linda. All the ways the bicep-bulging, money-golfing, Kansas-City real-estate-Hornet wasn't me. I got downright descriptive. Metaphorical. The story got away from me somewhere around dusk, and somebody, I think by the smells of the upholstery it was Cory, drove me home. I spent the night on the bathroom floor.

My mother used to say, a woman drinks to escape who she was, but a man drinks to become who he is.

When I woke in the bruised, blue dawn I felt empty of everything. Anger, frustration, resolve.

They were waiting for me the next morning when I came in to prep the Rotary luncheon. My head felt like a sack of hammers, and I was in no mood for the box sitting on the salad bar with my name on it:

"Dear Mueller," the card said. "We feel your pain."

As Sugarman, Cory, Regina and the morning prep guys watched, I opened the oblong box hopefully, expecting supersize Excedrin and a bottle of tequila, a banana nut loaf, a Linda voodoo doll, anything but what I found nestled in the crepe paper, staring back at me with one eye. It was about ten inches long and thick as my wrist, a jaundiced Anglo color, with an on-switch and two speeds.

I looked from Sugarman to Cory, to the line of hair nets, and back again. "I don't understand."

"Take back the night!" Cory said, beginning to laugh.

Sugarman cleared his throat. "You went on so long about your ex-wife marrying an animate dildo— We thought it'd cheer you up."

"Cheer me up? What the hell am I supposed to do with this?"

I picked up the box to toss the whole thing in the trash, but with the sudden motion a stabbing pain sliced through my head, and I dropped it, spilling the contents. Upon impact, the object suddenly switched on and began rototilling its way across the prep counter, sputtering and jiving until it ended, writhing, in the field green mix for the Ladies Auxiliary.

Cory responded quickly, picking it up with a pair of grill tongs and dropping it back into its cardboard coffin, where it sputtered under a fringe of frisee. As he did so, I noticed what I had not seen before, which was that they had named it and given it a slogan.

"Horny the Hornet," the box read.

The line guys were beside themselves.

"You guys and your wishful thinking," Regina scowled.

Cory and Sugarman stood there grinning. "It was that or a hand-gun," Sugarman said. "We went the way of metaphor."

Just that quickly, the object insinuated itself into our lives.

The entire staff overcame their reluctance to handle it right away, and over the following weeks as we worked on the Princess of Wales, the thing took on a life of its own. Everyone wanted to set somebody else up to find it, and we found it embedded in sacks of flour, staring down from industrial-sized cans of shortening, wearing a cape of croissant and propped next to the coffee machine. Who knows how many batteries were used. The Hornet's fleshy, beckoning gesture undulated tirelessly from apron pockets and trays of bread crumbs for more than a week.

I had to admit that it wore me out. It was a Wednesday, ten days before the wedding and about four jobs coming up besides. I was sitting with Sugarman and Cory at the break table, waiting for the last batch of brioche to proof while a tray of raisin tartlets browned in the oven. The drawings for the Princess of Wales were spread before us, and the object lay weighting one corner. It was not long before we ceased staring at the semi-circles and dowels of the drawings and concentrated on the object, that series of contours we'd come to know too well.

"It does sort of beg the question of who is the model," Sugarman said.

"Whose skin is that color?" Cory asked.

"We're becoming obsessed," I told them. "The thing has got to go."

"That's not what women want," Sugarman said, gesturing toward the object with a piece of doughnut.

"What women want? I'll tell you what women want. Women want ostrich boots. Women want the Sha-La-La nine-hole golf course in Kansas City Missouri," I said.

"I hope you're right," Cory said, still staring at the object. "Golf I can learn."

I donned an oven mitt and picked it up. Its weird color and strange ridges and plastic veins still made me wince. "This has gone on long enough," I said. "We've got a tough week ahead, and this is not helping. You can do what you want with this thing, but I don't want to see it."

"What do you want me to do with it?" Sugarman asked.

I've had occasion to reflect upon what I said next, the choice of the words, the implications for what would happen later. What I remember having said, as I dropped the object in front of Sugarman, was this: Put that in your cake and smoke it.

And just that quickly, our mascot and the focus of so many adolescent jokes during those challenging days, disappeared. I knew by the tittering laughter that the object was still around, but true to their word, I didn't see it, and I didn't think about it. I didn't think about Linda or the wedding. I thought about the extraordinary cake we were making and about what Linda had said. Don't let that cake become an obstruction.

What did she know?

Under Sugarman's skillful hands and Regina's sensibilities, the Princess of Wales had come into being in our back room on a scale and grandeur that even Bride Quarterly could not have imagined. Four feet tall if it was an inch, festooned with floral accoutrements in Linda's signature purple and teal. Sugar-pearled and candy-jeweled from base to bride. I allowed myself to breathe the sweet vanilla breath of the cake, and I felt something at the base of my neck between the shoulders unbridle and loosen. These ribbons and roses might be my last words to Linda. They seemed final. Fully formed, elegant, and right.

The day of the wedding, it was still early morning when we arrived at the Saffordville United Methodist Church. We drove breathlessly past fields hung in shrouds of mist. I remember the day now as clearly as if it were unfolding in front of me—bright, cloudless, perfect. Light breeze skirled the dandelions at the base of the steps as the event staff unloaded the cake from the truck. With each step I felt something in my chest pull tight as a stitch, the cake, moving like that, a frigate of flour and frosting.

Sugarman stood beside me, arms crossed over his chest. "Well you've done it now," he said. "How's it feel?"

I had spent so many hours during the last few days thinking about Linda's response to the cake, the hours of labor and love that would be nothing but an obstruction to her life. I had not stopped to consider how I would feel when I finally saw it there, our hours of work under the open sky. I thought of Sugarman's thick fingers pinching the marzipan curl of each rose. Cory-Pedro and I standing together under a sheath of spun sugar. All that work just for this. It was beautiful and horrible at once.

I took one deep breath. I was ready. "It's a fine day for a wedding," I said. "And wherever it is, I want you to put away that stupid object." I turned to Sugarman. "I only want to see one finger pointing today."

The look on his face told me what I had not thought to ask before. It was as we stood there waiting that I realized our mistake.

"You didn't," I pleaded.

"You told me to put it in the cake," he said.

"I was being metaphorical," I told him.

"So much for metaphor," Cory-Pedro sighed.

We stared at the cake, making its way up the church steps in the muscular grasp of the prep guys.

"Do you know—" I started to ask, but of course we all knew immediately.

The top layer, Regina had taught us, was traditionally set aside and frozen for the bride and groom to keep until their first anniversary. Making its way up the church steps, supported by the network of dowels and cardboard that formed the infrastructure of the Princess of Wales, underneath the yellow-haired bride and black-haired groom figurines, sat the twelve-inch round in question, festooned with marzipan roses, shaped sugar, and candied violets.

"Oh, no," I said to Sugarman.

"Oh, yes," he said to me.

Cory-Pedro said, "Oh, shit," and Regina said, "Serve from the bottom."

The next two hours were a blur of arrivals and seating, music and vows. I was so dreamily fixated on the cake and the implications of what it might contain that I failed to notice Linda entering the sanctuary under a veil the size of a bedsheet, later exiting on the bulging arm of her real-estate agent. Guests began to file into the reception area from the receiving line. Everyone in Linda's family pretended not to recognize me. Perhaps no one did. I stood with Sugarman and Cory near the cake, scooping balls of sherbet to drop into the punch. I was sweating profusely.

"I think the batteries are out. Nothing's going to happen," Sugarman said, but he was sweating too.

Linda looked at the cake once, for about a split second, as she and her new husband gripped the serving knife and beamed smiles into the camera. There was some flashing of lights, the usual smearing of cake on each other's faces, and they were off to the dance floor. I noticed that the groom, again, wore boots.

We served square upon square. We nodded through the appreciative oohs and aahs of friends and family requesting a rose or a piece of sugar sculpture. We worked our way through a stack of paper plates. We could hear the toasts, the chicken dance and the hokey pokey giving way to the throwing of the garter and the bouquet. Then, suddenly, Linda and her groom were gone under a shower of bird seed, strings of cans echoing their truck down the Kahola Lake Road. Guests continued to waltz. Older women fanned themselves with their hats, and the younger women carried their shoes by the straps.

I realized that I felt nothing at all.

Next to me, Sugarman had set down his serving knife and was proceeding to wipe his hands on a towel. He nodded several times, lips clenched in a thin white line. I thought I saw tears in the corners of his eyes. It was the damned cake, I thought. Carved into shambles. All that effort, and for what? This is when I saw Regina take Sugarman's big hand in her small, manicured one, and lead him onto the dance floor for the last waltz.

I started to speak to Cory, but he shushed me and watched his sister and Sugarman begin very slowly to sway in a box-step. "Will you look at that?" He smiled. "Surprise, surprise," he said.

If wishes were horses, my mother used to say, then beggars would rise.

"Not rise. It's ride," I told her once. "Beggars would ride."

"That makes no sense," she said. "Why would beggars want to ride?"

I sat at her bedside during the last moments of her life, holding her hand as I'd never done since childhood, waiting for the last words. I must say that I expected information about my father, that in her final breaths she would reveal to me the mystery of who I was as a man, and why I had failed. Her breath, steady, eyes bright, she pulled me to her with a surprising strength and asked if I would do something for her.

I told her that I would.

Dust, she said, and died.

She died in the house where she'd been born, in the bed where she'd been conceived, her secrets borne back into herself. Is it any wonder that all my relics are circular? Afterward, lifting rose-patterned plates and Hummel statuettes and wiping shelves, I searched the house for clues. I found nothing until, opening the silver drawer, I found not silver but wishbones. The tiny, clean-picked bones of birds she must have eaten over a period of years. Packaged in the sleeves for knives and serving spoons, only these brittle bones, these tiny stirrups, the unbroken wishes of my mother's life.

Linda's wedding ended something for me, but it was not the thing I planned. For years I had watched my own life play out behind me like so many ragged, frayed ends unraveling. I had waited for someone to tie a knot. Then two elderly ladies tottered past the remains of the Princess of Wales cake, holding each other by the arms.

The smaller woman wore a pink dress with white piping and carried a white patent leather purse. She stopped in front of Cory and asked after Mrs. Parsons. "The woman who used to cater your shop? She used to run a bake shop up in Melvern, you know. Before her troubles."

The other woman wore a mint-green pant-suit. She nodded in agreement. "Terrible business."

Cory smiled sympathetically and asked what we could do for them.

"You don't know the story, do you?" The smaller woman set her white purse on the cake table and cocked her head at Cory. "Poor Anna. I ran the cash register at the Duckwall's next door to her old shop. I was there the night she came into the bakery and found her husband after that girl."

The woman in green patted her friend on the arm. To Cory she said, "Parsons was a drinker. They were estranged. He used to break into her shop and steal the money out of the till."

"The girl wasn't more than sixteen," the small woman continued. "Not from around our way. Out of town. Emporia, maybe. No charges were ever pressed that I read of."

Conspiratorially, the woman in green whispered to Cory, "the rumor was always that she poisoned him, you know. Her husband. But that's a fib."

The woman in pink cut in again. "I was right next door. Shot him is what she did, Mrs. Parsons. She shot Mr. Parsons dead on the spot. Must have been the last straw, him doing what he did to that girl what worked for her. My brother was deputy then. He's the one told her to keep a gun in case of break ins. She must not of handled it much. Recoil busted her eye up something awful."

The woman in green agreed that it had. "Ugly," she said. "Turned it white."

Neither of them knew what had become of the girl. The smaller woman said she thought the girl might have gone to live with the Amish in Yoder, the kind of people who would take someone in her condition. Poor girl. No people of her own. Pretty girl, they both agreed. Round face. Blonde. She might have made out all right. The woman in green said what did it matter. It was a bad business.

I watched the two ladies totter together down the steps of the church into the sunlight and thought of my mother and Mrs. Parsons. A bad business, I thought. A sad business. I remembered the way my mother had set out the egg cup for Mrs. Parsons each night. The way Mrs. Parsons' flashlight looked on spring nights swinging an arc of light through the fireflies as she traveled the path that led through a pasture between our house and hers. I remembered the milk-white of her eye, and the way it seemed to me that the light of her lantern was a thread stitching the field, or a hunter flushing birds from the brush. There was a curious, child's rhyme my mother used to say as the flashbeam grew closer, Annie Annie two by four, crashing through the kitchen door.

At Mrs. Parsons' funeral my mother stood staring a long while at the raw new gash that would be Mrs. P's grave next to the slight declivity that was Mr. Parsons' thirty-five year-old one. The grave was weedy, a place I could tell no one placed flowers or wreaths of remembrance. And when she bent down over it, I thought my mother might brush away the milk thistle as one might brush a lock of hair from the face of a child. I thought she might dust the scrim of dirt from Mr. Parsons' stone. But what she did, bending over the sunken grave like that, was spit. It rolled down the stone, leaving behind it a trail of red soil. And when my mother walked away from the cemetery she never looked back.

Winters can be long around here, and I've spent this one thinking about everything that has happened. It's spring now, and Sugarman has moved back into town, with Regina. Cory is thinking about moving to Dallas to work in hotel management. We'll miss him, but I know he's destined for bigger things.

I live in the same house as always. Alone now. I go to work and drive home. I listen to radio through the screen door on warm nights. I walk the pastures with my dogs. They're good girls. Sugarman brought them to me, squirming pups. "Two blue heelers," he said, "to heal your blues."

He's a good man, Sugarman. But I don't think, any more, that I'm blue. Thanks to Linda, thanks to all of them, really, I know what I'm looking for now. When I find her, I will bring her here, to walk these places with me. There is always another chance at love, and this time, I won't try to tell her how the curve of her cheek opens a hinge in my chest. I won't describe the way the big Bluestem shimmies the hedgerow, or the double helix of swallows forming and reforming over the pond. I will take one of her hands in one of mine and I will watch for the quick intake of breath, the moment of surprise that says, Maybe this. Maybe you. And when I kiss her in the last blue moment of twilight or the slanting evening haze of summer, or the slatey scrim of a coming storm, when I kiss her she will hear my answer—Yes. Me, and the weather will change.

I've not heard from Linda again, but I have my versions of her story. In one, following the June wedding she gains sixty pounds and is divorced by September. Another version involves an anniversary fight, where she flings the still-frozen cake at her husband, kills him, and ends up in jail for the rest of her life, cell-mate to a woman named Martha. In the version I like best, Linda and her husband make it to the first anniversary and they find, when they cut the cake, the object we feared might be there. I can think of no better metaphor to tell her what I have learned to be true, which is that this life is nothing if not one strange and unexpected gift right after another.

About the Author

Professor **Amy Sage Webb** teaches creative writing, literature, literary editing, and pedagogy at Emporia State University, where she was named Roe R. Cross Distinguished Professor. She shares co-directorship of the Creative Writing program in the Department of English, Modern Languages, and Journalism. She has edited several literary journals, including *Kansas Quarterly*, *Hayden's Ferry Review*, and *Flint Hills Review*. She served as managing editor for Bluestem Press, and she continues to serve on the editorial boards of several presses, and as a reviewer for numerous publications, contests, and arts commissions. She serves as a consulting pedagogy specialist for Antioch University, Los Angeles, and has directed the pedagogy forums for the Association of Writers and Writing Programs. Her poetry and fiction appear in numerous literary journals, and she has been nominated for the Pushcart Prize. She lives with her husband in the Kansas Flint Hills.

www.ingramcontent.com/pod-product-compliance
Lightning Source LLC
Chambersburg PA
CBHW080837250626
47160CB00009B/2970